Washington Spring books

Here Lies

Book 2

D1518119

ROBIN ARCUS

ISBN-13: 979-8-77-619323-1
Cover design by: Art Painter
Library of Congress Control Number: 2018675309
Printed in the United States of America
All rights reserved.

ALSO BY ROBIN ARCUS

A Horse of a Different Color

IN MEMORY OF

JOHN AND ELLIE KETCHAM

WHO HAD A VISION FOR AN OLDER ADULT COMMUNITY

A diamond is one of the hardest elements on earth.
You can scratch steel with a diamond.
However, you can break a diamond with a hammer.
That is because a diamond is hard
but it is not strong.

1

FALABA, SIERRA LEONE
1952

"Shhh. He'll hear us."

"What if he finds us?"

"He won't if you keep quiet."

Nmumba gripped his younger brother's hands pulling them close to himself. He could feel both their hearts pounding.

"I think I hear him," Yusuf whimpered.

"Have faith."

Both boys winced hearing gravel underfoot. The smell of a cigarette penetrated the canvas under which they were hiding.

"Limey, get this truck moving!" a man's voice commanded.

"Right," a blonde-haired, middle-aged man named Liam replied.

Liam turned the ignition key. The engine sputtered. Both boys cringed.

When the motor started the boys blew out their breath into each other's faces. Neither opened his eyes. They remained cocooned in the bed of a pickup truck, soon to be miles away from their recently deceased mother, miles away from their grief and men they did not like. The boys knew they did not have the same father. They did not know specifically which man was their father and did not care to know. They cared only about each other and getting out of Sierra Leone.

For hours, the ten and twelve year old boys held onto each other feeling every ditch in the road. They longed to see the scenery. The truck bounced along washboard roads, the ribbed truck bed hemming them in and irritating their arms, hips and legs.

"Inspection!" shouted a voice as the truck came to a stop and rumbled in place.

"I have to poop," Yusuf whispered.

Nmumba sighed. "There's nothing we can do."

"How will we know when we can come out?"

"When we start to smell the sea. Then, when the truck stops in a very busy place, we can—"

Men's voices sounded close.

"I have orders from Vanderveld," Liam said.

The voices retreated. The boys said silent prayers.

Moments turned into minutes. Fumes leaked in under the canvas.

Nmumba started to cough. Now it was Yusuf's turn.

"Shhh—" Yusuf whispered.

"I can't help it."

"And I've got to poop."

Just then the truck door slammed shut. The driver shifted into first gear and the vehicle resumed shaking down the road.

"I have to get some air," Yusuf the younger mumbled.

The heat under the canvas was nearly unbearable. Nmumba, normally chiding said nothing. Yusuf unlocked his sweaty hand from his brother's and turned on his other side. He felt for the edge of the tarp and lifted it gently. A welcome breeze flowed in. Both breathed deeply as Yusuf continued to hold up the heavy material. Now longing for more than fresh air he moved his head to see beyond the truck.

"It's the sea!"

"Do you see it?"

"It sparkles! Oh Nmumba. It sparkles, like diamonds."

What do you know of diamonds, thought Nmumba. Neither had ever seen finished, cut stones that radiated brilliant light.

The boys had been born in Falaba into a loose confederacy of men who mined in alluvial pools for diamonds. Before they were ever conceived, their mother would walk from a neighboring town to bring food to her brother and collect the money he made from his mining efforts. It would have been more customary for a brother or a male family member to make these trips but there was no other male relative. The day her brother died she came to the mine pools unaware of her brother's death. The other miners trapped her and since no one came looking for her, they were able to keep her in their possession. They used her to cook their meals and bed down with them and she was powerless to stop their abuse. In time she bore two sons. She prayed her young boys would grow into men better than those who used her. But what other examples did the boys have? So their mother sang to them and told stories of good men who had respect for women. She also shared her dream that they would one day be free from Falaba.

"It's beautiful!"

The truck slammed to a stop. Yusuf fell back toward his brother. Their eyes searched each other wondering what could be the cause. They heard the truck door open.

3

"Git!" Liam shouted. "Git on, you goats!"

"How far are we?" Nmumba, the older asked.

"To the sea? Half a day's walk. Do you think we should go now?"

"Not yet. Wait until we're closer."

As the day began to wane they felt relief from the heat and hope build in their hearts that their plan would actually work.

Liam stopped the truck and shut off the engine. The boys heard the truck door open and shut. They could hear distant voices and friendly shouting.

"I want to look," Yusuf said.

"No. People might be watching."

Yusuf sighed.

Time went by. A damp coolness began to seep into their hideout.

"I think Mr. Liam has left for good. Maybe he left for the night."

"Maybe," Nmumba replied.

"Can we leave?"

Nmumba stretched his cramped body and made a decision. "Yes, carefully."

Yusuf the younger, slid to the very edge of the truck bed and slowly lifted the canvas. It was dark, but not impossible to see. They were outside of a town, pulled off in a remote area. The voices had been coming from a cluster of stalls now closed, some distance away.

"It's just us," Yusuf said.

"Go slow," Nmumba warned.

Yusuf undid his side of the canvas, slid out and rolled on top of it. He rose to his knees then stood. The sea was still in view. A few boats bobbed. And then he saw the ship. It was so massive his eyes almost didn't register it.

"Nmumba! A ship!"

"Shhh!" Nmumba scolded.

Yusuf folded back the tarp to free his brother.

"Look!" Yusuf pointed.

"What's this?" Liam's big voice and even bigger body appeared. He held a long-blade knife. "What are you two doing here?"

Yusuf, the younger looked at Nmumba as he always did to get them out of scrapes. But Nmumba was silent.

"Have you been in my truck since Falaba?"

The boys said nothing, believing if they were still then he would not hurt them.

"You two must be famished," Liam said, then smiled. He tucked his knife in a sheath then reached out to help Yusuf first. Yusuf looked quizzically at his older brother, his eyes asking if he should run.

"You're Yusuf and Nmumba, sons of Fatima. Let me get you something to eat."

Nmumba's legs were so sore and his stomach so empty that he didn't try to escape.

"Come over here." Liam had made camp near the truck. He motioned for the boys to sit. "Or maybe you want to stretch. We've been on that dusty road all day. What are you boys planning to do now that we're in Freetown?"

"We're not in Freetown," Nmumba mumbled.

"I bet you boys have never seen the sea. I remember my first time when my father took me to Dover. He talked about the War and so many lives lost. I couldn't imagine it with all that wonderful water wafting in and out." Liam pulled fruit and bread from his pack and gave it to the boys. "Seems to me you have some wanderlust." Liam picked up a stone by his feet and tossed it. "You want to be anywhere but those alluvial mines, is that it?"

Yusuf nodded, a mouth full of food.

"I don't blame you. I would do anything to avoid it." He chuckled. "That's how I got here. We had coal mines in my town. You want to talk about mines. Now those are mines. Real mining is going meters down into the ground, way down, so far down you're sure hell isn't any farther down than you are. Then you swing a pick ax and pull ore out of the walls. You toss it onto a cart and when you've got it full you start on the next one. Every day you pray the walls don't cave in. My father wasn't so lucky. He lived to thirty-seven."

Liam was quiet for a while.

"How'd you get here, Mr. Liam?" Yusuf asked.

"My mother's brother-in-law knew a man who needed a fetch-and-tote boy. My mother sent me to him and told me to do whatever he asked. I was thirteen then. I'm forty-four now. That's a lot of years of doing what you're told. Anyway, I wound up with Vanderveld delivering supplies. I make my rounds, including to Falaba." He paused, sizing up the boys. "What are your plans?"

"We want to go away from Sierra Leone. Away from Africa. To where you lived, Mr. Liam, to have a better life," Nmumba, the older, answered.

"How do you plan to get there?"

Nmumba pointed to the sea.

"It's a long way. Can't say as I'd swim. You could take a ship, but you have to pay for passage."

"We will work to get money to pay for it."

"I can carry things for people, like in Falaba," Yusuf announced.

Liam was silent, thinking.

"That ship leaves in two days for Tilbury Port in London. I need a favor and maybe you boys are the ticket. There's no leaving for me, but I need to get something to my sister in London."

The next morning Liam drove the boys into Freetown. Scents of every kind wafted through the air, acrid burning smells and pleasant cooking aromas. Chickens hung from stalls. Rice bread baked in clay ovens. Krio women hawked embroidered slippers. Everything shone brightly in the sun. The streets teemed with shoppers and merchants all trying to be louder than the other. Liam stopped the truck and motioned the boys out.

"I have some business. It's best that you stay with the truck. Guard it for me." Then Liam was gone.

People pushed by them trying to get somewhere other than where they were. At first the boys stood rigid, defending their plot of land by the truck. A truck was unusual since most passersby used carts and animals. A boy on a bicycle whizzed by and nearly knocked over Nmumba as if touting his superiority. By the time the sun moved to the other side of the sky Liam still had not returned.

"What are we going to do?" Yusuf asked.

"I don't know."

"I'm hungry." The aroma of food kept their mouths watering and stomachs grumbling, but they had no money.

"I will ask the lady for some food," Yusuf declared, pointing to one of the food stands.

"Why should she give you food? You have no money to pay."

"I will offer to help her. I can carry her things home."

"You will leave me here?"

"If I can get food, I will get enough for us both."

Young Yusuf did exactly what he said. He approached a dark, cheery faced woman who sold cooked chicken in rice bread, announcing that he wished to help carry her items home in exchange for food for himself and his brother. The woman laughed, her whole body rippling. Her smile showed a wide gap in her front teeth.

7

"You wish to help me?" she roared. "A small one like you?" She looked the lad up and down, from his coffee-colored feet to his black-haired head.

Yusuf nodded.

"Okay. I will need you to start now." She pointed to items and explained how to pack them. With chores completed she motioned for him to go around the bend to fetch her donkey. When he had everything loaded she produced two large packages of food.

"Take this to your brother. I will be waiting for you."

Yusuf grinned at her, feeling her warmth as she slid the wrappings from her hands into his. He hurried to Nmumba to share their feast.

Later, when Yusuf returned to the truck from his carting duties, he carried more food.

"She likes me."

"You are lucky that Liam didn't come back and demand that we leave."

"I wasn't gone long. Have you not seen him at all?"

"No."

"What if he doesn't return by dark?"

"Let's hope he does."

Night fell and the town quieted. Liam had not returned. The boys still stood by the truck.

"I am getting inside," Nmumba announced, daring to settle inside the white man's truck rather than return to the uncomfortable truck bed. Yusuf followed his brother inside the cab.

During the night Nmumba awoke to a grunting noise. He shifted positions thinking he was dreaming and then heard it again. Waking, he listened for the voice's direction. In the moonlight he saw a form crawling toward the truck.

"Mr. Liam," Nmumba whispered, darting from the truck to the man who was on hands and knees in the street. When he reached Liam, he could see that the man was badly bruised with both eyes swollen almost shut. "Mr. Liam, what happened to you?"

Liam could only grunt. Nmumba dropped to his knees and tried to help.

"No—" Liam whispered. "Don't touch me. It hurts too much." He groped on. When he reached the truck Nmumba wondered how to get the injured man inside.

"Thank you for staying," Liam mumbled.

"Maybe I can help you inside the truck."

"Let me lie in the ditch. I just need to sleep."

Nmumba looked for some way of creating a bed. He remembered the donkey and went in the direction his brother had gone. He returned shortly with arms full of straw. By laying it along the gutter at least it would prevent sewage from reaching Liam.

"Thank you," Liam struggled to say. Nmumba watched as Liam shut his swollen eyes and fell asleep.

Nmumba remained with Liam as dawn broke. Behind him the dark sky dissolved into a glowing pink and then white as the orange ball rose. He could see ahead of him the sun's effect on the water, glinting off the waves. Sea salt was the prominent smell until the hawkers and shops opened for business. People began appearing, shooting odd glances at Nmumba beside the blonde-haired man asleep on the ground. Nmumba felt himself to be a guard for this kind and wounded man. Yusuf appeared just as Liam began to stir.

"What happened to him?"

"I got on the wrong side of some blokes," Liam mumbled. His lip had an egg size bruise. His eyes and face were a mess. His hands appeared bloodied. "Fetch me some water from the truck," he asked.

Yusuf retrieved Liam's satchel and handed it to him.

"I want you boys to get ready for sailing." Liam raised himself to take a drink.

"That ship's the Manchester Star. It's a merchant ship, not meant for passengers, but you two can stowaway on board. Find where they're loading and just step in line to take the next load. Keep taking load after load until you feel like you are getting to know the ship. Every time you get on board, do what they ask, don't go anywhere else, but train your eyes to look for where to hide. When you can, slip aside and hide yourselves good. If they find you they may dump you overboard, so do not get caught. It will arrive in London in fourteen days, or in ten if the weather favors you. You will need to buy food to take with you. There's money in my right sock. Get it. The shape I'm in, I can't reach it."

Nmumba pulled out the pouch and handed it to Liam. Liam counted money and passed it to the elder brother.

"Now. My sister. I want you to take her this." Liam struggled to reach a pocket inside his pants. He produced a small envelope about the size of a coin purse. "She lives in the city of London at 14 Lancashire Landing." He pointed to the address on the envelope. "Her name is Winifred Forsley. Do not give this to anyone but her. That's very important. Tell her Brother Liam sent you and I will come when I can. I also want you each to buy a knife like mine," he indicated his other sock. "And don't be afraid to use it."

2

WASHINGTON SPRING
PRESENT DAY

"Acton, we will miss you." John B. Martin shook the hand of Acton Alexander and then pulled him into an embrace. "You have been more than kind to me. If it hadn't been for you this community may not have been built. When my wife was so sick and I couldn't tend to all the startup details for Washington Spring, you were here, checking behind the contractor, checking behind the builders and even the inspectors, making sure everyone was doing their job. Building twelve homes and bringing the project in on time was a credit to you. I'm just sorry to see you go. We all are."

"I am sorry, too, John. But it's for the best."

Acton thought of the money he had kept for himself from the sale of the stray pony. He used it to cover a fraction of his financial losses after his niece bungled his portfolio. He returned the money to Washington

11

Spring but not until after first embezzling it. John knew about his crime, as did Mary Gray Walterson, another of the Washington Spring residents. Acton was grateful John had not shared this with the other fourteen members of their community. Acton had reconciled himself to the fact that he could no longer be trusted, and decided to move out of Washington Spring. His million dollar entry fee was returned minus an amount for the time he had been residing there. That left him plenty of funds to find housing in Philadelphia near his younger brother. His story was that his brother needed him close to organize a campaign for public office. The truth was, Acton was leaving ashamed of himself.

Acton, the only black member of the Washington Spring community wore a crisply ironed shirt and slacks along with a tan, zipped windbreaker. He had grown emotional during his goodbyes at their monthly Community meeting. Now, he steeled himself not wanting a repeat of the prior evening. He and his rental trailer were packed and ready to roll. One of the advantages of living in 1,100 square feet was having less to move. Of that he had no regrets. He had also given away items to further lighten his load. To John he had given a book on military history. To Mary Gray he gifted a basket, small in size but huge in sentimental value, explaining he had purchased it on one of his visits to an artisan community in Africa. If he breathed deeply enough, he could still smell the sweet grass of Africa woven into its form. He gave it to her knowing she would appreciate the centuries-old skill passed from mother to daughter still in effect today.

Jimmy Johnson and Bryan Beal came out of their cottage and walked over to Acton to give him a final farewell.

"You better write and tell us you've gotten yourself settled," remarked Jimmy. "Bryan and I just hate to see you go." Jimmy's plaid pants and striped shirt shared little in common except for the color pink.

12

"You have been a real friend to us, Acton. Let us know when your brother wins his election," Bryan added. Bryan stood next to his partner, equal in height, but quite a contrast in gray pants and a gray sweater.

Acton boarded his car, started the engine and waved as he pulled out from his familiar parking spot.

The pertinent question for the Washington Spring members was who would occupy Acton's vacant home. For John the question was who would help complete the community's next project.

John turned to Bryan and Jimmy. "Building Willow Home will be harder now without Acton."

"It's too bad construction keeps getting delayed," Bryan said.

"So much red tape," John grumbled. "Most of my career I developed properties. We got Washington Spring built in nine months. This Willow Home project is taking longer than that just to get state approval."

Washington Spring was the brainchild of John B. Martin and his wife, Pauline, Annapolis millionaires. Their idea was to create a small enclave of active elders to care for one another through the aging process. The community was to be built in two phases: twelve independent cottages and later, a skilled care home. To support financial outlays both at the start and ongoing, each of the nineteen chosen applicants would provide a one million dollar entry fee as well as monthly dues. This purchased their house and the assurance they would be cared for until death. Applicants also had to be willing to share their skills as well as certain household items. Pauline would have had charge of the property's beautiful botanicals but she had died of cancer just as Washington Spring was preparing to live.

Washington Spring was located in rural Maryland in Parabar County outside of Parabar Shore, not far from the Chesapeake Bay. The Community's Phase 1, called the Washington Spring Close, consisted of a circle of twelve identical millhouses with eighteen total occupants. Phase 2 was to be a home-like skilled care residence for members whose health needs extended beyond the community's abilities. Willow Home would be run by professional health care providers employed by Washington Spring.

In addition to John B. Martin, the key personnel creating Washington Spring were Acton Alexander, Ben Lebowitz and Mary Gray Walterson. Acton had run Veteran Administration medical facilities and served at Washington Spring as project manager. Ben was an attorney able to advise John on legal matters. Ben's wife, Natalie, a former human resources director, would oversee the staff for Willow Home. Mary Gray Walterson, a retired assistant director of the National Archives, served at Washington Spring as chief correspondent. She also promised to keep a chronicle of their Community and to write a retrospective of their segment of rural Maryland. Mary Gray had started her research by visiting Richard Barclay, a descendant of the original William Barclay. During the 17th century, William Barclay, along with James Paramore arrived from England and founded the area by wresting it from the native Nanticoke tribes. Mary Gray had been diverted from her fact-finding in order to return a stray pony to its rightful owner. During that adventure she met an aging cowboy named Brown, who had taken to her like a bee to a begonia. At least those were his words. Now she wasn't so sure about his overt affection.

Glumly, John turned to go back to his cottage. Jimmy and Bryan feeling the same, also returned home.

"What did Brown say?" Bryan asked Mary Gray when they were at St. James-in-the Wood in the church's sacristy. Bryan, as the music director, was at the church to practice the organ for worship services the next day. Mary Gray as an altar guild volunteer was also preparing for

Sunday's services. Like Bryan, she was a resident of Washington Spring and a member at St. James Episcopal Church.

Mary Gray removed her polishing gloves, having finished cleaning the candle holders. "Brown said he wouldn't take no for an answer."

"What do you think you will do?"

"I'm not sure. Ever since Brown moved into Alice's place to take care of her farm, he has been after me to show him where I live. When we met last February in that snowstorm he was convinced that God had created it just so he and I could meet. He thinks God has been moving us toward one another and that we need to tie the knot. I am just so reluctant. When I'm with him I enjoy his company. He seems to love me more than anything. He fawns over me. He compliments me. He moved all the way from Richmond to Alice's just to be closer to me. But something is just not right." She stared at the gloves in her hand.

"Mary Gray. Look at me." Bryan took her gently by the shoulders and turned her toward him. He gazed down at her 5'4" frame and smiled. "You do not have to do as this man asks. You can trust yourself."

"He says he's coming to church this Sunday. Here. To St. James. And he wants me to bring him back to Washington Spring. I'm sure he wants to meet all of you. He knows that John and his wife Pauline were the creators of Washington Spring. He's heard me talk about Sue and Sandy, Tom and Tracie and Angelika. I told him that Angelika was heart-broken when Acton sold the horse. He wants to meet her since he's so fond of horses. I think I'm just going to have to bring him home with me. Maybe if he sees how small Washington Spring is, and that my house is only 1,100 square feet, he will realize that he is a big man who needs a wide open space, and Washington Spring is not for him."

"And therefore, you're not for him, either," Bryan finished.

15

3

LONDON
1952

Good fortune made passage possible in eleven days. The boys had enough provisions to remain successfully hidden, though they were exhausted by the trip and smelled as bad as the sewage hold they were near. When it was clear that the ship had docked, they stepped into view as though they were hired hands. However, their swagger evaporated when they saw how out of place they were. White faces met their black ones and men barked orders they could not understand. The boys scrambled to do as they were told, but they couldn't be sure what that was. After the first load they remained on shore trying to mix with the wharf crowds. Seeing a group of black men they rushed to them exclaiming greetings in their native Krio tongue. The men looked at the boys sternly and replied in unfamiliar words. The boys did not stop but kept walking. Mystified and miserable from so many days at sea, they tried to make a plan. This city was vast, far larger than Free-

16

town. The gay colors of Freetown were replaced by grey and brown. Trucks and other vehicles darted to and fro. The frenetic but friendly energy of the other port city was missing. Here men gathered in groups that looked more like gangs protecting their perches. Stares followed them as they walked and walked away from the sea.

"How will we find Liam's sister?" Yusuf asked. The two had laid down on grass in a park, astounded by this fresh, soft carpet of color. Yusuf looked at the sky as he said this.

"I don't know yet," Nmumba replied.

After a rest, the boys sat up and shared the last of their food. A man in a uniform appeared.

"Get on you ruffians," the man barked at the boys.

Not understanding, the boys smiled as if the presumed soldier was greeting them.

"I say, scat!" The policeman shouted.

The boys shrugged and continued munching on their meal.

Now the bobby grew upset and started toward the boys.

"I think he's mad at us," Yusuf the younger said. "Here—" Yusuf held out some of his rice bread.

The inflamed officer was going to say, *You think a little bread is going to keep me from evicting you*? But he had not had a thing to eat all day. His own circumstances were poor and his stomach was empty. He looked around to see if anyone was watching. Growling, he took the peace offering and ate quickly.

"You two are going to need to move on. This space here is for the public." His voice was softer now.

Yusuf, the younger, not understanding a word, simply smiled.

"Where are you tykes from?"

The boys looked back, uncomprehending.

17

Nmumba spoke to Yusuf. "Give him more bread. Maybe he can help us."

Yusuf handed him another piece of bread.

Nmumba produced the little envelope on which Liam had scribed his sister's name and address. He showed it to the officer. The officer made to take it away from him, but Nmumba held on tightly.

"You want me to show you where to find Lancashire Landing? Bread for directions, is that it?"

The policeman pointed the way talking in unknown words with Nmumba paying close attention to the man's gestures. From these he got a general idea of where they would need to walk.

By luck they found 14 Lancashire Landing but were unsure what to do. White men and women in fancy clothes gathered outside this very large brick house built close to the street. To those gathered, these two black boys looked strange and frightening in their bare feet and near rags. Conversation among the groups halted as one and then another took note of the interlopers. A black man in a suit opened the front door and a portly white man appeared. He spoke to the group, turning their attention away from the foreign youngsters. Yusuf and Nmumba caught the eye of the black man standing tall and still by the front door. They could see his eyes motion them to the back of the house. Nmumba took his brother's hand and they quietly slipped away from the crowd.

Finding the back of the house took some effort. Gardens and gates kept them zigzagging until at last they were behind the brick home. The tall black man met them and whispered a greeting. It was not their native tongue but similar enough to communicate. The man explained that he worked for the Forsley family. The boys grinned to hear the name Forsley as it confirmed they would be able to complete their promised errand.

18

"My name is Nmumba. This is my brother Yusuf. We come from Falaba. I have something to give Winifred Forsely."

The tall man's eyes widened to hear this African child speak the name Winifred Forsley.

"What do you want with Mrs. Forsley?"

"I have something from her brother. He asked us to deliver it to her."

"Give it to me and I will see that she gets it."

"I am to give it to her directly. No one else."

The tall man scowled. What would a youngster from Africa be bringing his mistress?

"You must give it to me," he insisted.

Yusuf blurted, "We can only give it to her."

"What's all this?" A woman's voice interrupted. "James, are we to understand that someone wants to see me?"

The tall man wheeled around, embarrassed to see his mistress by the back door.

"Madam, I am sorry these two—"

"Why do they come here?"

"They are to deliver you something from your brother."

"My brother! By all means, let them come!" She indicated for the boys to come to her. She was clean and extraordinarily dressed and now the boys became self-conscious. "Come, come," she urged. I want to hear about my brother! James, please stay and interpret."

"I don't speak their language, Madam."

"Surely you were just now communicating with them."

"I was trying, Madam."

"Boys, what can you tell me about my brother Liam? Do you know him?"

James attempted to relay Mrs. Forsley's questions.

19

The boys nodded. Nmumba spoke. "He said he will come as soon as he can."

James told her that her brother missed her.

Nmumba reached deep into his shirt and retrieved the little envelope. He held it out for Mrs. Forsley.

"From Liam?"

The older boy nodded not needing translation.

She took the envelope and smiled. She did not open it but slipped it inside her glove where it rested in the palm of her hand.

"James, give these boys some food. I must return to our guests."

She turned to go, then looked back at the two unlikely visitors she could never have predicted would come bringing a package from Sierra Leone.

That evening Winifred took care to undress out of view of her maid. She had been pressing her gloved hand into many people's palms since her serendipitous meeting hours earlier. She had been smart enough to place the envelope in her left glove, far less used, and therefore far less conspicuous. Now she was free to sit in her own bed chamber and discover what her brother had sent.

Gingerly she removed the pouch, smiling to see her name and address scribed by her brother's hand. Carefully she slit open the flap and pulled out a note. Unfolding it, two small stones dropped onto her lap. They were misshapen and rather dull. She then lifted the note to read her brother's familiar writing.

> *Dear Sister,*
>
> *Forgive my haste. Take these to Hatton Garden to the Morton shop. Speak only to Fredrick Morton. If this made it to you, then send the boys back to me. They will be the cord that binds us.*
>
> *+ Your Devoted Brother.*

20

Instinctively she checked behind her for witnesses, and seeing none, placed the two stones back into the note, folded it and raised it to her lips. She then returned it to the envelope, sat back in her chair and sighed. At last her brother was making himself useful.

Winifred often had calls to make during the week, so leaving the house with her driver was nothing new. Before boarding the car she tugged at her cloche to cover her ears against the damp.

"I need to call on a friend at Barts. She has been ailing and the doctors are having a devil of time with her. I want to bring her a reassuring word while she remains in hospital. This visit may take a while. One never knows what one will find or how long one has to wait. Please return for me at eleven-thirty."

Winifred exited the car and started for the front door. Confirming she was out of her driver's view, she turned away from the hospital and toward Hatton Street, glad she had chosen practical shoes.

A small bell tinkled as she entered Morton Jewelers. She was alone until a man looking to be in his fifties appeared. He wore an apron of the trade and a headlamp. He wiped his hands as though he had been at his workbench.

"I am looking for Mr. Fredrick Morton. Would you be he?"

"Yes, Madam. I am Fredrick Morton." The man shut off the light of his headlamp.

"My brother, Mr. Liam Lebroy asked me to see you."

The man did not register any recognition.

She pulled out the envelope from her purse. "He sent me these," she paused. Seeing nothing in the man's face she added, "from Sierra Leone."

The jeweler slid a dark velvet pad across the glass case in front of where they stood.

21

Winifred let the two stones tumble onto the smooth fabric as the jeweler turned on his lamp.

The next time Winifred met Mr. Morton she had four stones, all blue. She had paid for passage for the two boys to fetch her more diamonds and they had presented her with four one-carat gemstones. She had been reading about diamonds and knew that blue were most rare.

"I see you have brought me alluvial blues," he said, examining the stones. "The rarer, the better."

Winifred knew that her brother was building the Vanderveld business. He had made friends quite naturally with the men panning for diamonds because he brought their pay. But Liam always gave them more than money. He knew the value of cigarettes and liquor and these he gave out liberally.

4

WASHINGTON SPRING

"This is mighty nice," Brown exclaimed, removing his hat and entering Mary Gray's cottage. Six feet tall and more, he wore a clean shirt and slacks and offered to remove his boots. His Sunday boots, he called them. "You do have a way with things, Sweetheart."

Mary Gray followed him into her house, letter perfect in Wedgewood blue and white.

"I love how open it is," he observed.

Mary Gray wasn't exactly happy with the open floor plan design, but agreed to accept it since the space was so modest. Walls, though useful, would have crowded the rooms.

"Take me on the grand tour," Brown said.

"Well, you pretty much see it—living, dining and kitchen. Behind that door is the powder room. All twelve cottages look like this."

23

"You said it has two bedrooms and a main bathroom."

She led him to the sleeping part of the house. Mary Gray played the perfect hostess and after showing him views into her bedroom, the bathroom and the second bedroom which served as her study, they returned to the living space.

"And your screen porch?"

"It's out here. It faces the field."

They stood looking out onto the vast open land behind her house. It seemed too attractive, too appealing for Brown, and she didn't like that.

"It's a bit chilly don't you think?" she said. "Let's go back inside."

He helped himself to her sofa.

"I can see why you love it here. I would, too." He winked.

She sat.

"Sweetheart, I have been thinking. This business with the farm is at an end. I believe it's time for us to tie the knot. I am fool in love with you and the sooner the better."

"Brown—" Mary Gray started to speak. Would she tell him she didn't want to marry him? Could she resist this man's obvious affection?

"I know. I know. You are just too shy to say it. But I know you love me, too."

Mary Gray equivocated. "Our covenant agreement doesn't spell out bringing another person into the community. And if we were to marry, and live here, it would have to be approved by the Washington Spring community. They would have to vote on it."

"Then all the more reason I should be meeting these people now!" Brown got up from the couch and started toward the door.

Mary Gray didn't move.

"You still haven't told them about me, have you?"

"I told some of the residents." Mary Gray weighed her words carefully. "I told Bryan Beal. You met him today after the church service."

"Mighty fine fellow."

"And John knows about you." She didn't say that John only knew of Brown as one of two men who dug her and Alice out of the snow that entombed Alice's truck. Mary Gray made no other mention of Brown and perhaps had not even used his name.

The women had been on their way to pick up Alice's pony near Richmond when an epic snowstorm dropped its load and prevented Alice and Mary Gray from reaching the horse farm. Mary Gray feared that they would die from lack of oxygen, holed up as they were in Alice's truck. Thankfully Brown and another stable hand dug them out. Days later returning home to Maryland, Alice stabled her pony, came into her house and died. Mary Gray was left to help with the arrangements, including caring for Alice's farm. Brown convinced Alice's son that he was an experienced hand and could keep the farm running. And he did. But Mary Gray didn't feel entirely sure she wanted this magnanimous man, so large and lively, stuck on her as he seemed to be.

"Who shall we meet?" Brown asked.

A knock startled them both. Mary Gray got up, stepped in front of Brown and opened the door.

"Sue!" Mary Gray held open the door. Sue remained on the outside landing.

"You're alive. Good. I didn't see your bird so I thought I'd better check."

"Oh. I just didn't remember to put out my bird this morning. I was in a rush for church."

"Now Mary Gray. You know that your bird magnet has to be out on your door by 10 o'clock so the magnet monitor knows you've made it through the night. Just goes to show the merits of the system. Better to knock and know you're alive." Sue leaned her head in the door, now seeing Brown.

"You must be the owner of that Ram Charger out front."

"Why yes, ma'am." Brown came to the door. "The name's Brown Howard." He stuck out his hand to shake Sue's. Sue demurred as she took it, an uncommon response for her.

"Pleased to meet you, Mr. Brown."

"First name's Brown. Last name's Howard. I come from Brownsville, Texas. People started calling me Brown. Guess that's better than Wilford. And your name is?"

"Sue, Sue Cantelli."

"Pleased to meet you, Miss."

"How is it you two know one another?"

"We—" Mary Gray and Brown started at same time.

"You go ahead, Sweetheart," Brown said.

"Brown was one of the men who rescued Alice and me in that snowstorm outside Richmond. He joined me for church this morning and has come to see Washington Spring first hand."

"You are a true hero," Sue said. "So you live in Richmond?"

"Once upon a time. Right now I live in Halifax County in your fair state, and run the farm where Mary Gray's friend Alice lived. I'd like to live even closer to Mary Gray." Brown looked her way and smiled.

"I see," Sue said, taking in the scene. "I hope you will enjoy yourself. Will you be staying a while?"

"As long as this little lady will have me." Brown grinned.

"Well, welcome then," Sue said. "I best be getting back to Sandy, my husband. I asked him to do some chores for me. You two have fun!" Sue turned to go.

"Well, she seems pleasant," Brown announced as Mary Gray shut the door.

5

LONDON
1952

"I say, Old Chap. I must have something to soothe the breast of my dear young wife. She is not in favor of making this move tomorrow. If you ask me, her mood has more to do with leaving that lover of hers she thinks I don't know about. It will do her good to be free of him. And I am tired of playing the fool. Fresh start in America. That's what it's all about. At forty-seven I should think I could still make a killing. Never marry someone twenty years your junior. I thought it would be easier than this. Show me something nice, very nice."

Fredrick Morton motioned his cousin to the back of the shop.

"Something special have you?"

Fredrick slid open a drawer and showed him a large diamond he had completed cutting.

"Take a look." Fredrick handed his cousin a loupe for closer examination.

27

The man held it to his eye. "Why it's brilliant!"

"Look at how it refracts the light."

"Amazing, Old Chap! Now, all I need is a setting worthy of this brilliant gem. What do you suggest?"

"I would say a pendant, something next to her heart."

"I agree! And the larger, the better. Can you do it now?"

"It will take the day to do it."

"Wonderful. Just enough time for me to make my last rounds."

6

WASHINGTON SPRING

Mary Gray decided her house needed a deep cleaning. It would be a convenient diversion from her confused thoughts. One moment she imagined herself tethered to Brown and the next she shuddered to think of it. People liked to say to follow your heart. But she didn't know her heart. After a failed marriage in her twenties, she focused her energies on work. At the National Archives she rose as high as a woman could. She resented that she always had to be on guard about the men around her. The lower ones wanted her job, her peers felt her unequal, and her superiors she had to carefully cultivate as mentors. She had used her mind, abandoning her heart and now her heart was a stranger. Oddly, the person who seemed to know her heart best was Bryan. The two had become fast friends during Washington Spring's construction. He seemed to think she did not love Brown and had no problem telling her. She had to admit, if she were to describe her ideal life partner, Brown was not it. He was too much like her father, a man she adored as much as any little girl could. Her father would sweep her into his arms, call her his loveliest daughter and shower her with gifts. He also broke her heart.

Mary Gray and her mother were so much alike. Medium in every way. Medium height. Medium weight. Medium brown hair, at least when it was brown. Nothing distinguished them, and therefore her mother felt that her husband so big, handsome and full of life, was an unlikely catch. Mary Gray thought of how her mother busied herself throughout the week waiting on her husband to arrive home each Friday. During spring-time especially, she would polish the furniture and reline every kitchen cabinet and dresser drawer. The house always smelled fresh. "If you clean the corners the rest will take care of itself," she often said. Mary Gray therefore decided to begin by emptying her corner cupboard. This piece of furniture was among her most prized possessions, built by her father while they lived in Millidge, Vermont.

Mary Gray cleared her coffee table and scooted it toward the corner cupboard to unload its drawers to replace the liner paper. Her relocation to Washington Spring more than a year earlier had meant a stringent process of weeding out items she absolutely did not need. This brutal off-loading still haunted her. Here in her new home she would start walking to a drawer only to realize it contained none of the items it once had. However, before moving she had not cleared the corner cupboard since it contained few items up for debate. She lifted the first drawer and turned to place it on the coffee table. Pivoting she tripped and though she caught her balance, the drawer flew from her hands knocking into the coffee table as it fell. The drawer's bottom splintered.

"Damn!" she shouted.

The drawer and its contents splayed across her living room floor. Getting to work, she moved items to the coffee table and then picked up the empty drawer. The wood had fractured across the bottom.

"This lasted all these years and now I've ruined it." She felt nauseated. The drawer had been angled to fit perfectly into the narrowing corner cupboard. It would be hard to fix.

"What's this?" Mary Gray spotted something on the drawer's broken bottom. A manila envelope had been taped to the underside. Carefully, she removed it, put the drawer aside, and sat down on her sofa.

Undoing the envelope's clasp she pulled out a thin cloth-bound book. She also found a much smaller envelope. From that envelope she extracted a square of thin parcel paper. Carefully unwrapping it, her eyes flew open. Four brilliant blue diamonds rested inside along with a tiny slip of paper that read, *Return to ME*.

"Diamonds!" she exclaimed. Mary Gray then puzzled over the words. *Return to ME*. Did they mean for the receiver to return the gems or for the receiver to return him or herself to the giver? The handwriting appeared to be her father's, but with only three words it was hard to tell. Her mind raced.

Her father had been in mining his whole life, a managerial position that she could never understand. He was gone during the week but always home on weekends. His mines were gravel and granite. He had nothing to do with diamonds. Or did he? He certainly never spoke of them. She turned over the jewels in her hand, then held them up to see the colors refracted by the light. Brilliant fire red from blue gemstones. They were exquisite. Mary Gray felt caught in a world of mystery. She placed the four diamonds back in their little wrapping paper.

Next, she opened the cloth book and began to read.

7

WASHINGTON SPRING

"B en?"

"Over here," Ben called.

"I couldn't see you," harrumphed Natalie, his wife, catching up to him. "I've got several morels and look at this beautiful lion's mane. What have you found?"

"Not mushrooms. Look." Ben pointed to a partial jaw bone protruding from the earth.

"Is it human?"

"Not sure."

Ben took a small hand shovel from his kit and sank it into the ground making wide cuts around the bone. His shovel hit something solid and broke.

"Oh my god! There's more," Natalie exclaimed.

Ben stood up and leaned back to survey the site.

"What do you think it is?" she asked

32

"I'm not sure."

"Do you think you should dig it out?"

Inside her cottage, Mary Gray sat on her sofa mesmerized. *E. Morton* was written in script on the inside cover of the book. Mary Gray carefully turned the page.

May 20, 1953

My husband, dear man, gave me a gift, a pendant he had set for me. Had he known the hands making it were the very hands I dreaded leaving, he would never have paid his cousin to make it for me. Imagine my surprise to see that Fredrick had created not just a pendant but a locket—one that opened from the back. And when I opened it, to my astonishment, four blue diamonds appeared, wrapped in a briefke.

May 31, 1953

My heart aches to think of Fredrick alone in London. I wear his locket all the time. My husband interprets this to mean he is the keeper of my heart. I admit to you, Diary, that I married my husband to be close to Fredrick who would not marry me. The day we met I was shopping for a gift for my sister. For me it was love at first sight, something about his manner, his blue eyes, the warmth of his smile. He shared his loupe so I could see up close the gemstone he recommended. And when he touched my hand, it was fire.

September 26, 1953

I convinced my husband that I must make a trip to London to see my mother. I had to see Fredrick. He makes me so happy. We ate kippers from a can and drank wine until dawn. When I was with him he told me that the four diamonds came from Sierra Leone. He said that Winifred Forsley has two boys working for her who make frequent trips to Africa. Fredrick buys diamonds from her. I wore my locket and little else that visit. He asked if I would ever part with it. I told him I never would.

June 17, 1954

My heart is full of grief and fury. The London Times wrote that Fredrick was killed—a thief invaded his shop and stabbed him. An investigation has begun. Oh, how I hope the killer will be found. The news is more than a week old since my newspaper deliveries are delayed. I showed the article to my husband and asked if we will go to London for his cousin's funeral. He looked at me strangely and said he didn't care to. It would seem very odd if I expressed interest in going.

August 17, 1954

My husband's heart attack came out of nowhere. Both of my Morton men are now gone and I am lost. My days as a Morton widow bring me nothing but grief. The payments I was promised by the firm have stopped and I cannot find anyone to tell me why. I depend more and more on the generosity of others.

September 28, 1954

Today I met a wonderful man. His name is Bill. How unlikely that I would meet someone so tall and handsome. I was sitting in the park, wondering what my life would become when this handsome man with a mustache appeared. He just came strolling by and took a seat beside me. I didn't know whether to laugh or cry. He has a big nose and volunteered to tell me he had it broken during the war, but he said that was all that broke because he stayed behind working here in the States. He asked to see me on Thursday evening. I believe I will tell him yes.

October 6, 1954

Bill is darling. He talks constantly and makes every story seem real. True or not, I feel alive when I am with him.

34

November 11, 1954
Bill has advised me to sell the house and buy something more practical. I am
accustomed to a certain standard of living, but must admit to my circumstances. I will
buy a lovely but sensible home.

December 14, 1954
Bill comes by every chance he has. His work keeps him so busy, the weekends
especially. I am fortunate to see him on the weekdays. He makes this small house
joyful.

January 7, 1955
I may be in a predicament.

January 29, 1955
I am in a predicament. I don't know whether to tell Bill. I keep thinking he will
propose which would make this predicament legitimate. Why won't he propose?

February 14, 1955
I have no one to talk to but Bill. He is my world. I wait for him on Mondays and cry
to see him go on Fridays. I think he knows something is wrong.

February 23, 1955
I told Bill. He said he can't marry me. I am desperately depressed. He told me that
he is already married. He said I am the love of his life but he has responsibilities he
can't walk away from. He tells me he will provide for me and for the baby. He says it
will be okay. But it is far from okay.

March 5, 1955
I am sick, so, so sick.

August 31, 1955

Everything is almost ready for the baby. I hope Bill will be happy. I try to be as happy as I can.

September 3, 1955

I have a girl. Ursula Ellen Morton. I am forced to wait for Bill to contact me. I feel so alone. A moment like this is supposed to be shared. I am too young to be a widow and without a father for my daughter. There is little provision to pay for her and our lives here.

January 18, 1956

Bill has been paying for everything. We would starve without him.

September 3, 1956

Bill was here for Ursula's first birthday. I loved looking at him look at her. She looks like him and it pleases him tremendously. I do not ask about his other family. We are his family.

January 30, 1957

I love Bill so, but I do not enjoy charity. I asked him to sell Fredrick's pendant. I need the money. I also asked him to take my diamonds for all his gifts to us. His eyes grew large when he saw the four alluvial blues. At first he refused them. I told him I didn't want them. They make me feel vulnerable. He finally agreed to hold them for me. When he saw them he told me that diamonds are one of the hardest elements on earth, that you can etch steel with one. He also said that you can break a diamond with a hammer. He said that is because diamonds are hard but they are not strong. He told me he did not want my diamonds to come between us—it would be like a hammer to his heart.

April 6, 1963

It's been six years since I wrote. I lost my diary. Bill comes every few weeks. This week he was here. He makes like we will be together forever, but I know it's not true. When he sees Ursula he wheels her around. He even held her up in the air. She's getting a little too big for that. But she loves it. She loves him.

Mary Gray dropped the book into her lap. Her twelve-year old self had been right. Her father had another daughter. *Ursula 1963* had been written on a picture she had pulled from her father's wallet. The day her life changed. Until now it was supposition. Today it became fact.

8

WASHINGTON SPRING

"Leena, it's been ages. How are you?" Ben pulled the 70-year old woman into a light embrace. He set her back and held her by the shoulders to give her an assessing glance. "You haven't changed a bit."

"And you're a good liar. Natalie, he always was a good liar." Leena called out.

"I know." Natalie came from the kitchen to greet Leena. The women hugged. "How are you?"

"I'm fine, but you're a long way from civilization."

"Oh, not really. Parabar Shore is our post office. We have a grocery store and hardware store for small things. We ride into Annapolis every two weeks for the big stuff. It's fine, really. We love it here. But enough about us. Tell us about you, Miss Fully-Retired!"

"I know. I never planned to work this long, but time flies. And besides, Cornell was ready to replace me with someone younger and more athletic."

"Usually means cheaper and dumber," Ben added.

"Come sit down." Natalie motioned Leena to the sofa.

"So these are your new digs. Comfortable, if you like this sort of thing. I had you two pegged for a high-rise in upper Manhattan."

"When Ben retired, his younger brother convinced us to live on the Chesapeake Bay. He had a rental he was tired of dealing with and offered it to us at a reasonable price. We thought that would be our happily-ever-after home."

"But then Natalie saw an ad for this place." Ben picked up the conversational thread. "They were just forming Washington Spring and prospective members were invited to apply. We could downsize into a newly constructed home with sixteen other people and feel like we were part of something. The idea is to look out for one another as we age in place."

"Do you get to play lawyer here, Ben?"

Ben laughed. "Something like that. I did get my Maryland license. So far there hasn't been much call for my skills. We all had to have our e-states in order as part of the application process. You should do something like this, Leena."

"Maybe. My first order of business is to figure out where to put fifty-six boxes of books. Being an anthropologist does require heavy lifting."

The three laughed.

"Seriously. Do you think you will stay in Ithaca?"

"I really don't know. Teaching has always been my first love. I can't imagine not having a class to prepare, or papers to read or some committee meeting to attend—or avoid."

Again, they laughed.

"We have missed seeing you," Ben gushed. "Leena, what was our motto when we were all at NYU? `Give a little, take a lot. Look out world, Greeks we're not.'"

"I'll drink to that," Natalie announced. "Ben, would you get us some drinks?"

"What can I get you from our special supply? You name it, we probably don't have it." He chuckled.

"Just a glass of wine, white if you have it."

"Coming up."

"When we all lived in that walkup on West Houston I thought the day would never come when I would graduate from NYU, and look at us now. Natalie, you thought you wouldn't pass biology. I remember quizzing you at night."

"Biology was never my thing. Give me people. Give me numbers. Now you're talking my world."

"That's why you made one heck of an HR manager," Ben bragged. He handed glasses to Leena and Natalie and sat down across from the women.

"So what do you two do with all your time, now that you have time?"

"Ben's been doing some birding. We're in an amazing place for birds," Natalie said. "He's even got me looking through binoculars. We are on a migratory route for most everything that flies."

Ben added, "When we lived right on the Chesapeake I grew interested in the water and therefore the birds. You know the Chesapeake has salt and fresh water. Every kind of life is there. It's fascinating."

"I'm going to check on dinner." Natalie rose and took her glass into the kitchen.

"Seems like you would have all kinds of life around here. Do you get deer and fox?"

40

"We do. We had a stray horse for a while," Natalie offered from the kitchen.

"What's this?" Leena picked up one of two pieces of bone on the coffee table. She held it up to the light. It was dark with age. "Where did you find this jaw bone?"

"Ben and I were mushroom hunting the other day a few miles from here." Natalie appeared and placed a tray of hors d'oeuvres on the coffee table near where the bone had been. Leena put down the fragment and looked at Ben.

"You know it's human."

"Is it? I wondered. Do you think I should contact someone?" Ben asked.

"Yes—" Leena looked at Ben like it was obvious he should have known better.

"Even an attorney can learn something new every day." Ben leaned from his chair to swipe a cracker through the dip.

During the evening Leena implored Ben and Natalie to take her the next day to the site where the bones were discovered. Now she followed the two as they retraced their steps from their mushroom foraging trip. Leena wanted to investigate the area and had along a kitchen sifter, a trowel and a collection bag.

"Wasn't it around here?" Natalie said, pointing to a stand of trees.

"I think it was more like over here," Ben pointed in a different direction.

"You two aren't much help," Leena chided.

"What do you want us to look for?" Natalie asked.

"The most important thing is to remember where you found the bones."

They spread out and walked within sight of each other.

41

The three were silent except for the sounds of their feet tromping through the tall grass.

"Here!" Ben exclaimed. "I found my shovel." The women hurried over. "My hand shovel broke when I was digging. I can't believe I found it."

Grass waved over the area. Except for some roughed up dirt where Ben had been digging the prior week, there was little to distinguish it from any other part of the field.

"I'm going to establish a site perimeter," Leena explained. "When we start to dig, we need to go slowly, tread the area carefully and save all the dirt. We will sift it for bone shards and other types of fragments."

"What other fragments would there be?" Natalie asked.

"Knife blades. Bullets. You never know."

A week later Natalie and Ben sat on their sofa listening to Leena on their speakerphone. She shared her lab findings.

"The original jaw bone and the additional bones we found indicate this was a male. Unfortunately, I can't establish age. The bones are tremendously deteriorated, consistent with being in the ground fifty years or more. I can't tell you more at this point. But I am satisfied that more digging won't bring us further results. I will work with what I have, at least until they kick me out. It's good to have professor emeritus privileges here."

Ben looked at Natalie who looked at Ben. "Thank you for trying. We'll be on pins and needles to hear more," Natalie said.

42

9

WASHINGTON SPRING

"I need to take these altar cloths to the church and set up for tomorrow's services," Mary Gray announced to Brown. "While you're gone I'll look at that porch door of yours. You don't need cold air leaking into your house. Feels good to have Saturday chores."

Mary Gray was in no mood to talk Brown out of his plan. Besides, getting some distance would clear her head. He bear hugged her as she left and then began to retrieve tools from his truck. Inside the cottage it didn't take long for him to tighten the upper door hinge. After several test swings, he congratulated himself on an easy fix. Tools returned, he sat on her sofa and looked around for something else to do.

"Bryan, what do you know about diamonds?"

"Mary Gray! I didn't know you were here at the church." Bryan turned around to look over the top of his reading glasses. In his late

43

sixties, he remained trim and kept his scarce hair closely cropped. "I guess I'm a little focused on tomorrow's service." He held a pencil in his hand along with Sunday's bulletin. "What did you ask?"

"Do you know anything about sourcing diamonds?"

"Precious little, I'm afraid. Why?"

"My father had some, but I'm afraid they may be ill-gotten."

"What do you mean?"

"My father was in mining his whole career. But he was in granite and gravel. Not diamonds. Besides, there's only one diamond mine in the U.S., in Arkansas. I don't think these came from there."

"Leave it to you to do your research, Ms. National Archives."

"I may have worked for the National Archives, but mining was not my area. I'm afraid these stones came from Africa as part of a smuggling operation. Probably the Vanderveld syndicate."

"What makes you say that?"

"Vanderveld had exclusive operating rights in Africa. And I believe my father's diamonds were from Sierra Leone. Apparently Vanderveld enlisted youngsters to help with smuggling. These diamonds were probably secreted into London and from there into the hands of the Morton family."

She waited for recognition. Seeing none, she continued. "The Morton family was known for dealing in diamonds and weapons." Mary Gray raised her eyebrows awaiting his reaction.

"Diamonds and weapons? Should we be worried?"

"I'm not sure. No one knows I have these, except you."

"Well I'm certainly not going to tell. No matter who tries to torture me," Bryan said with a laugh.

But neither felt the humor in his remark.

~~~

"The Residence Review committee has asked for time on today's agenda. Natalie, would you bring us up to date?" John B. Martin asked.

The Washington Spring members were gathered at founder John B's cottage for their monthly Community meeting. Mary Gray took notes on her laptop. Around the room everyone focused on Natalie.

"We have a preliminary application for Acton's vacated cottage. The applicant has groundskeeping skills and is willing to assume all the outdoor work. Ray, that would relieve you of the grass cutting, trimming and planting as well as plowing and shoveling."

Ray Miller tilted his beer can toward Natalie in acknowledgement. "Wish I could say my back was better."

John chimed in. "As you all know, none of the landscaping companies we've tried has worked out."

"The applicant also has the requisite million dollar entry fee as well as suitable financial stability to cover the monthly dues, and because he does not have property he's needing to sell, he is prepared to move here as soon as possible. The Residence Review Committee met with him and has unanimously voted in favor of accepting this candidate. We now look to you for confirmation."

"What is his name?" Angelika asked.

"Wilford Howard."

Mary Gray gasped.

"He prefers to be called by the name Brown Howard."

How had Brown managed to apply for Acton's cottage, meet with the committee and raise a million dollars, and without her knowing?

"That name sounds familiar," Sue said. "Mary Gray, is that the man you've been seeing?"

Mary Gray's heart raced. She felt cornered. She stammered, "Yes, Brown Howard is the man who has been looking in on me. He was one of the men in Richmond who rescued Alice and me from the snow-storm."

"He's quite a gentleman," Sue cooed.

"Yes, he mentioned that to us in our interview," Natalie went on. "His profile is printed on this handout for you to read." Natalie passed out papers.

PROFILE

Name: Wilford Howard

Current address: 7634 Suffolk Rd, Halifax, MD 20649

Age: 67

Marital Status: Widowed

Primary Language: English   Other Languages: None

Education: University of Texas, B.S. Ag Science

Occupations: State Agriculture Extension Supervisor, Ranch Foreman, Stable Manager

Interests: outdoors, animals

Skills: Animal and landscape management, handyman

Health insurance: Medicare + Supplemental + Part D

Reason for applying for Washington Spring membership

My parents taught me that contributing to the welfare of others grows the heart of a person. I guess I could use some growing of my heart so I would like to contribute to Washington Spring while I can still be of use, and enjoy the people who are part of it.

Allowing time for everyone to read their page, John then resumed the meeting.

"Hearing the recommendation of the Residence Review committee are there any questions before we put this to a vote?"

Mary Gray wanted to object but couldn't form a single word of protest. Bryan caught her eye.

"Will we have a chance to meet Mr. Howard before we vote?" Bryan said, trying to stall.

"The Committee asks for a blind vote to ensure a non-prejudiced outcome," Natalie replied.

"This fellow sounds great!" Ray said.

"Then, hearing the recommendation of the Residence Review committee, all in favor of accepting Wilford Howard as the next resident of Washington Spring, please say *aye.*

"Aye," said voices around the room.

"Are there any opposed?"

With his eyes, Bryan implored Mary Gray to say something, but she remained mute as she recorded the vote.

"Hearing none, Washington Spring accepts Wilford Howard as our next resident."

Mary Gray wondered if she would throw up.

"Sweetheart! Have you heard the news?" Brown was on the other end of the telephone an hour after the meeting.

"Yes. How about it?"

"Ms. Natalie called and told me just a few minutes ago. She said the cottage is available any time for me to move in. I am thinking of next Saturday. The last of the animals is being relocated this week. Did I tell you? The boy is getting Sally May. That father of his may have a heart, after all. Said he's got a barn lined up outside of Baltimore so the boy can see his beloved pony whenever he wants. I've got to close up shop here anyway, and end of the week is as good as any. I can pack my kit and be over to you quicker than a bee on a begonia."

"Brown, I don't mean to pry, but I didn't realize you were so well set, financially."

"Darling, there's more to me than you know."

Why did she think that was true.

John B. answered a knock at his door. Bill Worthington from Cottage 4 stood on the landing.

"Bill, what can I do for you?"

"Can I talk to you for a minute?

"Sure, come in."

The two sat at John's table.

"What's up?"

"Christine has started wandering, John. Her confusion is worsening."

"I noticed at the monthly meeting she seemed agitated."

"I've been sliding furniture in front of the doors so she doesn't try to leave the house. It comes and goes. That's the thing. Sometimes she's clear-minded. She's aware that she's not operating on all cylinders."

"How can we help?"

"I'm not sure there's anything for anyone to do but me."

"You seem tired, Bill."

"I don't sleep very well. It's like Chris used to say about the kids when they were out, she'd sleep with one eye open. I think I know now what she meant."

"It has to be wearing on you."

Bill sighed.

"You came here because you knew we could deal with this together. Would it help if someone stayed in the house overnight?"

"You mean instead of me?"

"How about in addition to you?"

"We've been sleeping in the same room which is hard but it's also good because when she gets up, I usually know it."

"How often does she get up in the night?"

"Three or four times. We used to joke about the kidney and bladder crew working overtime, never letting us sleep. But it's more than that. It's her general restlessness. She gets up, walks around the house. I lay in bed listening. One night she was in the kitchen starting to cook something. That scared me."

"If we took turns, just as an experiment, staying the night—"

"It would be a tall order—to remain awake all night, just in case."

"Maybe we would take shifts. What time do you go to bed?"

"Eleven o'clock. She likes to sleep in, though, and I have to say, when morning comes, I'm exhausted and I sleep as late as her."

"What if we had an eleven to four shift and four until nine shift? We can discuss it at the next Community Meeting and create sign ups."

"I have to say, it would be a relief."

"Mary Gray can you pick me up on your way to St. James for church tomorrow morning? Jimmy totaled our convertible," Bryan explained through his phone next door.

"He what? Is he okay?"

"He's fine. The car's not. It's going to be an insurance nightmare. He says it was the other person's fault. She says it was his fault. Both were turning into the same lane at the same time."

"And the car's totaled?"

"Well, that's what the insurance adjuster is going to say—that the value of the car won't be enough to make repairing it worthwhile. Since Jimmy and I have been splitting the car between us, I don't have a way to get to church."

"What about practicing? Don't you usually practice the organ on Saturdays?"

"I do, but what little practice I did earlier in the week will have to suffice, unless you're going over yet this evening. Do you have any altar guild work to do?"

"Actually, I do. I can pick you up in twenty minutes."

"What will you two do for a car?" Mary Gray and Bryan were in her car on their way to St. James.

"I've actually been thinking that Washington Spring should start a car share program. We could have vehicles to sign out as needed. One could be a pickup truck. Another could be an SUV. Maybe electric cars."

"That's forward-thinking of you. How would the insurance work?"

"I don't know, but universities do it. Townships do it. Why not us? Speaking of insurance, did you get extra insurance now that you have those diamonds?"

"I didn't even think about it, Bryan. Do you think I should?"

"Can diamonds catch fire?"

"No, but if the place burned down they would certainly be lost in the rubble. Do companies insure against stuff like that?"

"I imagine they do. You'd probably have to add a rider to your homeowner's policy. Call your agent and ask."

Monday morning Mary Gray looked around and decided she loved her warm, inviting house. It was the right size. It had the right feel. It would be too small if Brown lived there, too. She was glad he had stopped asking her to marry him. In fact, he had not called her for several days; neither had he stopped by, even though he was practically next door. That seemed odd. He must be busy getting adjusted to living here, she thought.

Assessing her to-do list she saw the words *Call Insurance Agent.* She looked up the number and dialed.

"You will need to get an appraisal so we can write the policy to reflect the jewels' value," the insurance agent said.

"Where do I find a jewelry appraiser?"

"Annapolis has listings. Call one or two and see what they tell you. They'll need to see the diamonds and write out an appraisal form. When you get that, scan a copy to me so I can give you a quote."

Hanging up the phone Mary Gray went to her jewelry box to look again at these things of beauty. Lifting the lid, her eyes fell on the spot where she had placed the diamonds. They weren't there. She shuffled the items that were there, rings, pins and bracelets. She stooped down to feel the floor. Nothing. The diamonds were gone and she had nothing to prove that she had them. Her heart lurched. Her mind went immediately to Brown. Brown must have found them. And sold them.

"Bryan, the diamonds are missing." Mary Gray snapped up her phone and dialed, then tried to remain steady and sound calm.

"What!?"

"I did what you said. I called my insurance agent and he told me I need an appraisal before he could write a policy. When I went to my jewelry box they were gone."

"Did somebody take them? Were other things missing?"

"No. Nothing." Mary Gray suddenly realized that Bryan was the only person she had told. Why was she so quick to blame Brown. She could be talking to the thief.

"Who else knew you had them?" Bryan asked.

"Nobody."

"Mary Gray, please don't think that I—"

"I'm sure you didn't. Did you tell Jimmy about them?"

"No."

"Honest?"

"Queen's honor."

Mary Gray sighed.

"Was anyone in your cottage?" Bryan asked

"Larry brought over the vacuum cleaner, but I was with him the whole time."

"What about Brown?"

"That's what I'm thinking. He was here two weeks ago. After all, how did he come up with one million dollars to buy into Washington Spring? It adds up," Mary Gray said.

"Huh. What can you do?"

"Good question. I can't prove it. I can't even prove I had them."

"Maybe you need to ask him."

"What would I say? Did you steal my diamonds? He'll deny it."

"Did you ask him where he got the money for Washington Spring?"

"He said he has more resources than I know about. Something like that. He was a bit shifty. Now I know why." Mary Gray shook her head in disgust.

"Should you tell John?"

"And say what?"

"A thief is on the loose. You think it may be Brown"

"And therefore?"

"Well, I don't know. He shouldn't be trusted."

"He's John's latest favorite, now that he does all the outdoor work."

"I don't know what to suggest you do," Bryan concluded.

"Can we have the agenda, Mary Gray?" John B. Martin asked.

The Washington Spring members sat tightly together in John's cottage with John at the head and Mary Gray at a right angle to him at his dining table. Others were at the table and those who didn't fit occupied seats in his living room. Washington Spring did not have a central gathering space which was a point of consternation for most members.

"New business is a plan for helping Bill and Christine at night and a proposed car-share program. The other business is to send around the signup sheet for bird duty this month," Mary Gray said.

"We also want to introduce our newest Washington Spring resident," John added. "I know you all have been anticipating our newest member. Some of you have met him. He's already been hard at work around the Close. But for those who haven't, it gives me great pleasure to introduce Wilford Howard. He says everybody calls him Brown."

Brown began in a loud, Texas-twang. "They call me Brown because I'm from Brownsville, Texas." Mary Gray noticed he was wearing new boots. "I am in charge of groundskeeping, and I look forward to those responsibilities."

"We're glad to have you with us. Do you need anything to help you get moved in?" John asked.

"I'm all in and happy as a hog in a wallow."

John nodded. "Our new business pertains to Bill and Christine. I asked them not to be here so they wouldn't feel awkward about our discussion. Christine's been getting up at night, sometimes going into the kitchen to cook, and at times she tries to leave the house. Bill and I talked about ways to support them at home since we don't yet have Willow Home built, not that her needs are so severe. Bill and I came to the conclusion that Washington Spring members need to stay with them at night to be sure Christine doesn't wander off or fall or turn on the stove. I proposed to Bill that we could experiment with two shifts each night, eleven to four and four until nine in the morning."

Everyone was silent.

"Mary Gray has a clipboard to send around for everyone to sign up for two shifts per month. We formed this community to see one another through the aging process. This is our first real opportunity to do that."

"Dementia doesn't affect the brain the way most people think. When a demented patient begins to wander it's generally because they—"

"Sue, I'm sorry to interrupt but we have other new business to discuss."

Mary Gray grinned to herself that Sue was being shut down from one of her lectures meant to demonstrate her vast nurse's knowledge.

"The other new business is the topic of implementing a car-share program. Bryan, would you care to explain your idea?"

"Thank you, John. Jimmy and I, being without a car, began thinking about how little we actually use one. Obviously, we need reliable transportation and some of us are still working, but I've done an informal study of how often the cars in our community are actually driven. It's less than you might think. Jimmy and I want the next car we buy to be available for the community."

"You work a lot of the time," Ray Miller scowled, his Miller Time insulator sleeve wrapped around his beer can. "When would this car of yours be free for us to use?"

"We would only drive it certain days so others can have a chance. And maybe we could eventually have a car-share program. If Washington Spring had several vehicles, we would have enough for all of us. And like other things, we learn to share."

"How many cars are you talking about?" Ray asked.

"I would like to conduct a survey and find out more about everyone's transportation requirements. Right now this is just a preliminary idea."

"Please give us your assessment, Bryan, will you?" John asked.

"Happy to," Bryan replied.

~~~

"Anything to report?" Brown asked in a hushed voice. He stood hat in hand inside Bill and Christine's cottage facing a fatigued and lounging Angelika.

"It's been quiet, actually. I think they are both sound asleep, where I want to be. This is harder than it seems, staying awake when you have to. I say I'm an insomniac, and don't often fall asleep until way after midnight, but having to stay awake is another story. I thought that reading would help, but I think it's what made me sleepy."

"Your book must not be very good."

They both laughed.

"Are you settled in your new house?" Angelika asked, now sitting up.

"Happy as a pig in clover." Brown sat down.

"It's not an easy adjustment. At least it wasn't for me."

"Oh? Why's that?"

"It's a long story."

"Looks like we've got time."

Angelika brushed back her white blonde hair. A German accent lingered in her speech. She looked at Brown, then down at her hands.

"I was living in Denver in a house I loved, with a garden I enjoyed tending. And then my 90-year old aunt in Annapolis got sick. Actually, she fell in her home, broke her hip. She had no one but me, so I came east thinking it would just be a few weeks after she came home from the hospital."

Angelika shifted her gaze to Brown who looked at her with intensity. His mustache twitched.

"After six months I realized this wasn't a short term arrangement. I was trying to help her regain her strength and agility hoping she could continue living alone. I'm a physical therapist by training. But I think I was too optimistic." Angelika sighed. "My aunt also required a lot of other help. She had a large home and yard and I couldn't keep up with everything. I don't know why I ever thought *she* could. In the meantime, I lost my house in Denver."

Angelika looked down, embarrassed.

"The mail at home was piling up. My neighbor occasionally sent it to me. I finally filled out one of those forwarding things for the post office. What I didn't know was that the mortgage company's correspondence wasn't being sent. I knew I was behind paying them but I didn't realize they were planning to foreclose. It was a mess. My neighbor called me one day and asked if I knew that movers were taking furniture from my house. I got on the next flight and found the locks had been changed and my house had been emptied of all my belongings."

"That's a shock," Brown said.

"You can't imagine. I had family heirlooms from Germany dating to the 1600s. The family Bible is what I miss most." Angelika's voice trailed off. Then gathering herself she continued. "I had to reconcile myself to living in Annapolis. So, I changed my address, my license, all those things and started to think of myself as an Easterner. That was hard."

Angelika's eyes met Brown's.

"I'm from Texas. I understand," he said, nodding affirmatively.

"That's right. You're from Brownsville."

"That's why I'm called Brown. Real name's Wilford. My parents called me Will, but once I got to trail living, people started calling me Brown."

"I grew up in Texas, speaking German," she laughed. "My grand-parents were from Germany. They came to the States when they saw that World War I was about to break out. They had relatives who had settled in Bulverde, near Fredricksburg, so they were able to go there. My father grew up here in the States. He became an engineer and mechanic. Uncle Wenner went into the military and my Uncle Ernst was a farmer and horseman."

"A horseman, you say?"

"Uncle Ernst. Yes. He and Aunt Mechtild had a farm and I loved staying with them. Most of my summers I spent on their farm. My uncle taught me to ride."

"Ah, so you're a seasoned rider?"

"It's been a long time. When the pony showed up here I wanted us to keep her. I was the one who worked with her and looked after her."

"So Alice had you to thank for looking after Sally May. You know, I'm the one who moved into Alice's after she died. I ran the place. She had a barn full of horses, including Sally May."

"Who's taking care of the pony now?"

"Alice's son had her moved closer to their place near Baltimore. He said he found a farm to stable her. I am glad to think that Alice's grandson will still get to ride his pony. You know, that boy had never been on a horse. Said he was too scared. But the day of his grandmother's funeral I got him on Sally May and that boy was a natural. He said he never knew how great it could be."

"I sure do miss riding."

"Hey, I have an idea. Why don't you and me see if we can find a farm with some horses and go for a trail ride?"

"I would love that! Hadley Jackson owns Jackson Stables on the other side of the county. Maybe he would let us ride."

"That was the most fun I've had in years!" Angelika exclaimed.

"Seeing you happy makes me happy."

Brown helped Angelika down from her horse. He stood half a foot taller as she turned to face him. He leaned toward her and brushed away

a fly. Angelika felt his heat. Now close to one another she said conspiratorially, "I want to do that again."

"And you shall!" Brown announced, pulling away from her and their
intimate moment.

In his truck on the way back to Washington Spring they saw a trail-
head sign by the road.

"That must be the North-South trail," Angelika said.

"What's that?"

"Runs through the state of Maryland. I found it by mistake one day. I
like to walk and—"

"Whoa Nellie!" Brown slammed on the brakes.

A bear lumbered across the road fifty feet in front of Brown's truck
and disappeared into the trees.

"I've never seen a bear in these parts," Angelika said with wonder.

"This time of year the young are trying to establish their own ter-
ritories.

"That was beautiful."

"Black bears are beautiful. Do you get them at the Close?"

"No. You probably noticed we keep the dumpster carefully closed."

"I did see that. I was going to say let's check out your trail, but maybe
you don't want to, now that we know bears are on the loose."

"Actually now would be the perfect time. Maybe we will see it again,
or its brother."

"Look at that clearing," Angelika said. Brown had parked the truck
and they were following the trail for fifteen minutes.

Brown plopped down in the grass and then laid back to look at the
sky. Angelika did the same.

They were silent for a while.

"See those big clouds? Those are cumulus clouds."

"That one looks like a walrus."

"Looks more like a bear to me," Brown rolled over and play acted like he was attacking her.

Angelika play acted screaming. "Mr. Bear. Please don't hurt me."

"I only eat the ones I like," he said in his best bear voice.

"Then please don't like me, Mr. Bear."

"But I DO like you," he said, and in a swift motion lowered himself on her and met her lips with his.

10

WASHINGTON SPRING

"Anything happening?" Angelika asked Mary Gray. Angelika plopped down on Bill and Christine's living room sofa.

"Christine came out here around 2:30. She asked what I was doing. I said I was reading. She took it on faith and didn't ask me why I was in her house in the middle of the night. I asked if she had come out for a glass of water. She said yes, which offered her a good cover story since I'm not sure she knew why she had gotten out of bed. So I got her a cup of water. We sat at the table for a few minutes not saying anything, and then she said she was going back to bed. Haven't heard a peep since."

"Good to know. Mary Gray, I've been meaning to ask, are you and Brown a couple?" Angelika didn't know how to bring up Mary Gray's relationship with Brown. She had heard from Sue that they were seriously dating. Angelika knew her question sounded abrupt, but she didn't know how else to ask. And the two didn't often have reason to make idle conversation, even though they lived across the Close from each other.

"Friends. We're friends," Mary Gray answered.

"You told me once that you had been married."

"Many years, ago, yes."

"Were you happy?"

"Yes. No. I mean, I don't think anyone marries with the idea they will be unhappy. My husband was a very bright man. But he couldn't seem to turn his brilliance into a good job, at least one that he liked. It frustrated him. He ended up selling appliances at Sears. It was hard on him to see me in a paying position in our same field." She paused and chortled.

"He couldn't see the headaches I had at work because, after all, I was working in my field of choice, so to him these should have been tolerable. I couldn't really talk about them for lots of reasons, including that so much of my frustration was how the men at work treated me. My husband would have taken their side. So, I kept things to myself. Meanwhile, he grew more and more disillusioned with his job at Sears. At first he could make light of his teaching skills and intellectual prowess being put to use to instruct housewives when to use hot or cold water washes. He also didn't like that he wasn't the bigger breadwinner."

"That must have been hard."

Mary Gray was quiet.

Angelika spoke. "My husband died when I was fifty-seven. I was glad I had gone to physical therapy school. I would have been financially devastated otherwise. Thank goodness by that point our son had finished college, although we had co-signed on some of his student loans. My son's field was marketing and his first job was with a travel agency. It went well enough, but he was also living in San Francisco, so he never seemed to have enough money to cover rent as well as his loan payments. You can guess who ended up paying those." Angelika's face broke into an ironic smile.

Mary Gray nodded, as if in sympathy.

Angelika thought about her marriage. It had been tolerable, maybe even better than most. Given their German compatibilities, she and her husband understood each other and had the same need for cleanliness and organization. But emotions were something they didn't much share, so she really didn't know how deeply her husband's feelings ran. For all she knew he may have had a lover. She also didn't want to know. What she did know was that she had spent most of her time raising their son and managing house and home. Which is why she was open to Brown's advances. She had not been with a man who was so openly affectionate. It felt new and, if she were honest, exhilarating.

"You didn't have children?" Angelika then asked.

"No."

Angelika now nodded, as if she understood Mary Gray.

"Children are not always easy," Angelika admitted. "I lost my house in Denver. The irony was that I kept paying my son's student loans, but I didn't pay my mortgage. I could juggle everything when I was working, but when my aunt in Annapolis fell and broke her hip, I came east to help her recover. It took months of rehab and even then she didn't fully regain use of her legs. In fact, she ended up having a stroke, which is what took her. She was an amazing woman. She was a war bride, born in Germany. She met my uncle when she was in Belgium. She was fleeing the Nazis." Angelika absently twisted a button on her blouse.

"Sounds like quite a fortunate meeting," Mary Gray said.

"My uncle was what they called a Ritchie Boy. These were young men, Americans, who spoke German. Most of them were one or two generations from the old country, but full-fledged Americans. Since they had German language skills and knew the culture they were trained to be spies and to get information from captured German soldiers. Their training camp was right here in Maryland. Camp Ritchie. I think that's why after his tours my uncle wanted to return to Maryland and not to Texas. Besides, this part of Maryland looks a bit more like Germany, at least the part where our family came from. Compared to Texas, that is."

Angelika smiled and went on.

"My uncle was also at the Nuremberg Trials. His job was to get high-ranking German officials to disclose secrets they knew about the Soviets. You probably remember at the start of World War II the Soviets backed Germany. It was only when Germany invaded Poland that the Soviets switched sides. The U.S. generals figured that these high-level Germans knew Soviet secrets and it was my uncle's job to extract them."

"That was probably the safest he ever felt, in his pursuits."

"Not really. Undercover KGB were also in Nuremberg and could have created an accident, if you know what I mean."

"I'm sure you're right. It's amazing the Allies were able to recover the art and artifacts the Germans had confiscated during the War. Items are still being recovered and returned today."

"Yes. Hitler had been running his war machine on the gold he stole from the countries he occupied and used it for arms and weapons. Such a travesty, turning a country's own currency and wealth against its own people."

Both woman looked down, as if mourning the dead.

Angelika continued. "Hitler had his war spoils hidden in German banks, most of it in Berlin banks near his headquarters. When it became clear that the American's were about to invade Berlin, Hitler ordered the loot moved to mines. The biggest one was—"

"The Merkers Mine," Mary Gray finished.

Angelika stopped short of saying that some of those high-ranking German officials her uncle interrogated disclosed other loot piles, private purses siphoned off from the Merkers mother lode. Some that her uncle had kept.

A bed creaked and a sleepy Bill appeared. "Making a trip to the bathroom. Thank you both for being here."

In a few moments the toilet flushed and Bill shuffled back to the bedroom.

"Well, I hope you have a quiet rest of the night," Mary Gray said to Angelika. Mary Gray picked up her bag and started for the door.

Through her night watch Angelika thought about the money that had bought her a place in Washington Spring. She certainly felt guilty that some of it came from her uncle's pursuits. She reasoned it served good purpose now by keeping her off the dole. And hopefully her son, too. Weren't these positive outcomes? She had to admit that being a member of Washington Spring gave her a secure feeling, knowing she would have a safe haven through the rest of her life. That is, if the fates allowed.

"I'm serious! Let's get us a tent and go out to that patch and sleep under the stars." Brown leaned over and stroked Angelika's face. They were sitting on the couch in her cottage.

"Tonight?"

"Tonight."

"Where are we going to get a tent on short notice?"

"The hardware store in town has some. I bet I can get over there before they close. Pack a few things. I'll throw some food in a cooler and we'll be under the sky like it was meant to be."

"You make it sound like an adventure."

64

"Sweetheart, with you it certainly will be!"

"Put your stick *near* the flame, not *in* the flame." Brown wanted to show Angelika he knew how to cook a hotdog.

"I *have* done this before."

"These buns are toasted just right." Brown stooped over his make-shift grate and slid the buns onto a paper plate. "The beans are about done, too." He fished the can from the fire ring he built and stirred the gooey contents with a plastic spoon. "Nothing like camp smell on beans."

"My dog is done. Hand me a plate."

"Here you go." Brown handed Angelika a plate with a bun. "Scoop up some beans. I got us some potato chips. Open up the bag and help yourself."

They sat back and munched on their meal. Brown was right. There was nothing better than eating under the wide open darkening sky.

After they ate, they sat by the dwindling fire talking.

"What did you think of Denver?" Brown asked.

"I loved it, especially before it became the megalopolis it is today. It used to be just a big western town, an oasis of civility between the open range and the Rocky Mountains."

"What took you there?"

"My husband. He was also German and wanted to attend graduate school. University of Denver offered him a scholarship and he asked me to say yes to him before he said yes to them. So I did, and the rest, as they say, is history."

"Seems like there'd be more."

"We both worked hard. Maybe too hard. He died of a heart attack in 2015. We have one son, Christopher. He lives in California. After I raised him, I went back to school to become a physical therapist. I was able to work in my field until my aunt had her accident and I came to Maryland." She poked a stick into the fire until it caught and blazed. "I miss Denver, I really do. You really liked riding the range, didn't you?" She looked up at his face. His features were alternatively shadowed and revealed in the firelight.

"Those were my best years. They were my hardest years. But that's when you learn who you are. When you're tested. It's why I still get up with the dawn." He tossed a handful of dirt on the fire. "And speaking of dawn, I'd say it's time to turn in, wouldn't you?" He looked at her, a smile under his mustache.

"I'll beat you into the tent!" Angelika jumped up and sprinted the twenty yards. Brown, not as nimble, met her a few moments later.

"You're like a gazelle!" he said. "But I'm a bear, and bears like gazelles." He pulled her to him.

"Come out with your hands up."

"What in tarnation?" Brown's muffled voice returned.

"This is the Parabar County Sheriff. Come out with your hands up." A bright beam suddenly lit the front of the tent.

"Sheriff, we are indisposed," Angelika called out.

"I repeat. Come out with your hands up." The light remained.

The sheriff heard rustling noises and then Brown crawled out of the tent with Angelika behind him. They stood wrinkled, white and naked in the sheriff's expansive light.

"What in God's name?" the sheriff sighed. "I thought you were kids! Go get your clothes on." He shifted his spotlight to the field.

Brown and Angelika scrambled to pick up their hastily thrown-off clothes that were scattered outside of the tent and then ducked back inside.

"When you're dressed come out here."

Brown and Angelika shortly reappeared and stood in front of the tent.

The sheriff powered down his light and strolled to them. "Now what do you two think you're doing? This is private land. The owner called me and reported a fire and kids messing around back here."

"We thought this was part of the North-South trail. We thought we'd have a little campout tonight, sleep under the stars." Brown tried to sound reasonable.

"The trail runs through private land. There's simply an easement for thru-hikers. That doesn't include camping. Look, I'm going to have to arrest you for trespassing."

"Arrest us?"

"It's not that big of a deal. Look, it's more like a fine. You'll have to pay it and agree not to do it again. But I have to take you to town and report it to the Magistrate. Strike camp and get your belongings so we can go."

11

WASHINGTON SPRING

Brown and Angelika were silent on the drive back from the Magistrate's office. She had never been so embarrassed in her life. She wondered if something like this would be reported in the local newspaper. She felt utterly humiliated being called out by the sheriff. Brown remained quiet about the whole affair.

"Let me make it up to you," Brown finally said, breaking the chilly silence. "Let me get you some plants for your pots. I know you like to grow things and the best way to put something to bed and forget it is to grow something new."

She was quiet.

"Come on, what do you say?"

Angelika loved plants, and flower pots were as close as she could come to something like large-scale gardening. She had fantasized about asking John if she could be the Close's gardener. Brown was clearly in

68

charge of groundskeeping for which she was grateful since she had no desire to mow grass or shovel snow. But planting and tending, that she could do. And for a little while, she thought she and Brown could make a pretty good outdoor team. Given the last twenty-four hours, she wasn't sure she should do anything more with this man.

"Please?" he said in his best bear voice.

She couldn't help but smile. "Okay," she finally relented.

"Good. We shall go tomorrow and buy you as many begonias and black-eyed susans as your big bear can carry."

While strolling through rows of plants at the nursery Angelika's cell phone rang. She sneaked a peek at the number to see if she should answer. Christopher was calling, but he would have to wait. Angelika's heart ached to talk to her son but she wasn't prepared to answer just now.

"Let's get some of everything," Brown boomed. He rolled a cart toward her while she let her phone surreptitiously slide back into her pocket.

After check out, Brown moved plant trays from the shopping cart into his truck. Slamming shut the truck gate he smiled at Angelika. She noticed his mustache twitching above his lip.

Back at Washington Spring the two unloaded plants and bags of soil by her front door. When he left, Angelika sat on her front steps and listened to her voicemail.

Closing her phone she felt sick and sad. Her son needed money. Even though he didn't say it, she knew. Mothers always knew. She had made the mistake of agreeing to co-sign on his San Francisco condo, a good buy he said, and promised to refinance in two years to take her off the mortgage. But two years had come and gone and his finances still weren't working. Neither was he. The condo had belonged to his friend

Stevie, who herself had been in a financial fix. Stevie had talked Christopher into buying her out. After all, they both occupied the home and neither could come up with a better plan. Back then Christopher was working. He had contract work, enough to get a mortgage if he had a co-signer. Stevie had counted on Christopher to save them, though Stevie was temporarily in Chicago seeing her mother through the end of her life.

What Angelika didn't know was that Christopher had received a foreclosure notice. He hadn't told Stevie or his mother. He was in such financial straits that his heat was off and he had resorted to shoplifting food. He even kept an eye on the city bins for leftovers tossed out as trash. Christopher had joked with his mother he might one day show up for a visit and not to blame him if he stayed. When Christopher made the call, he held his cell phone to his almost completely covered ear, trying not to shiver in spite of his jackets and blankets. He didn't want his chattering teeth give away his condition. He tried to sound casual with his message.

"Hi Mom, just checking in. Give me a call when you can. Love you."

Angelika had a heavy heart. She threw herself into gardening hoping Brown was right. She could use something good to replace something bad.

For a week she worked hard, planting begonias, black-eyed susans and diamond frost euphorbia in her front yard. Out back she created a bed for shade-loving plants and groundcover. She filled flower pots for her porch and more for inside. At the end of the week she still had more flower pots than she had rooms. But it had been worth it. Digging into earth was always worth it.

12

SIERRA LEONE
1953

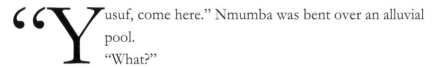 "Yusuf, come here." Nmumba was bent over an alluvial pool.

"What?"

"Look—here—"

"What is it?"

"I think I found what others are looking for."

Nmumba gingerly handed his brother a stone.

That night Nmumba and Yusuf lay outside under netting to avoid mosquitos. The moon had not yet risen and stars appeared like sparkling pin pricks shining through dark velvet. Growing up outdoors the boys were always aware of nature as they breathed in the familiar scent of West African air.

71

"After this next trip we should stay in London," Yusuf, the younger, said. "We know the city and enough of the language. Besides, Mrs. Forsley treats us well."

"She treats us well because we bind her to her brother. Do you see how she looks at her black servants? She does not regard them as equal," Nmumba said.

"We may not be equal, but we are important to her," Yusuf counter-ed. "She pays our passage so at least we don't have to stowaway and risk being caught."

"We won't be important to her if we no longer smuggle Liam's diamonds." The boys had long ago figured out Liam's scheme.

"We will make her think we can serve her better by staying. Or we can become sick when it's time to return," Yusuf said.

"But that only buys us time."

"Why not just sell the diamonds for ourselves, the ones Liam gives us and the one you just found?" Yusuf asked.

"And then what? We don't know the diamond trade. We don't know how she turns them into money," Nmumba said.

"We can follow her and see what she does. And do it, ourselves."

"Little brother, you really think a white man will buy diamonds from us?"

"Someone will."

72

13

LONDON
1954

"You idiot! Why did you kill him?"

"He was going to kill you!"

"Oh my god. Let's get out of here." Nmumba motioned his brother to follow him.

"This way," Nmumba's panicked voice called. The two raced down Hatton Street and turned at the next corner.

"You couldn't see that he had a gun. He was going to shoot you."

"But why would he have shot me?" Nmumba said.

"He didn't trust that you had something to sell to him. He probably thought you were a thief."

They were going over the events just past, now that they were blocks away.

"I didn't know what it would be like to kill a man. Oh my god, there was blood everywhere. Liam wanted us to have knives so we could fight anyone on the ship. I didn't think I would need it here."

73

"We can't go back to Mrs. Forsley's. It will be obvious something's wrong. We can't be connected to this," Nmumba said.

"Don't you think it will be more obvious if we *don't* return to her?"

"That's a chance we'll have to take," Nmumba declared. "We will sail to America."

"America?"

"Yes, America. It is the land of the free."

"Free in what way?"

"No hardships. Not like here. People are equal there."

"When can we leave?"

Down at the docks the boys had become savvy about which men were more trustworthy. None were, but some were better than others.

"You want to know which liners cross the big soup?" The London dockhand pointed to the water with his chin. "Where do you young mates want to go?"

"America," Nmumba replied.

"Where in America?"

"Anywhere," Yusuf chirped.

"The Allan Line runs the royal mail. Puts in at different ports. If it don't matter, then take any of 'em."

"When does she sail?"

"Thursdays."

The boys haunted the docks by the Allan Liner. They watched with seasoned eyes to see how the ship was loaded.

"I think we can do it, Nmumba," Yusuf said optimistically.

They had learned the skill of careful observation and how to fit in. Down at the docks all manner of skin tones were common. What was more exceptional was their youth. But they were older now. Nmumba was nearly fourteen and Yusuf was twelve. Their growing bodies would make stowing away easier because they looked slightly more like deck hands, yet more difficult because hiding their bigger bodies would be harder.

"We will sleep with the mail sacks." Nmumba declared.

"It will be hot."

"We've had worse." And they had. On their first passage from Sierra Leone to London they had hidden in a crawl space next to the sewage hold which was both impossibly hot and odorous.

On the Thursday of their departure, before dawn, Nmumba and Yusuf fastened their wax-papered provisions to their bodies, slipped into the water, and swam for the ship. From watching, they knew they could board by the rudder.

14

BALTIMORE
1954

The ship crossed the Atlantic in seven days, reaching port in Baltimore. The two boys waited for the engines to shut down. The near silence hurt their ears. Carefully, they began creeping their way toward freedom and went ashore.

"You boy?" A middle-aged black man called to Nmumba.

"My name is Nmumba," Nmumba said in his native tongue.

"You speak no language I know."

"My name is Nmumba," Nmumba repeated, now in his fair British English.

"Where you come from?"

"Falaba. Sierra Leone."

"And you just now got here? Some of us has been here a lot longer than you. My granddaddy probably from there. No telling. And why'd you come here?"

"My brother and I, we want freedom."

"Freedom—you come lookin for freedom here?"

"Yes."

The man shook his head. "The rest of us be wantin to go back to Africa."

"Our mother is dead. We have no one. We came here."

"Mighty brave boys. Who's your brother?"

"Yusuf," the younger boy answered.

"We want to work."

"Do you now? What work do you do?"

The older boy shrugged. "What is there?"

"Railroad jobs goes to whites. Crab pots and oysters to Polaks. If'n you can cook or clean, you might get somethin. Won't be much."

"What do you do?" Nmumba asked.

"I work at a garage. I work for a white man. Don't we all."

"Can we work there, too?" Nmumba asked.

"What do you know about cars? You ever seen one?"

"I drove one," Yusuf bragged.

"Now that's a tale. Don't be telling me tales, boy."

"I tell the truth. Liam let me—" Yusuf started until Nmumba cut him off.

"We can learn if you teach us," Nmumba said.

"Look, it's not my garage. Carry these parts to my truck. I was down here to get parts for a Volkswagen I'm working on. You probly don't know what a Volkswagen is."

The boys shook their heads.

"It's the latest thing. Man pulls in with his brand new car. I says `Where do I put the gas?' He laughs. This car isn't like any other car. You got to see it to believe it. Looks like a bubble can. But he says it's the next big thing. I's thinkin, this is the next small thing. So he comes by every Friday for gas and now that I know where to put it, I start askin where'd he git it? He say he bought it right here in Balmor. It's German. I's thinkin, we just beat them Germans. Why's we want to buy stuff from em? But he say it's gonna be the new wave. Last week his car come in on a dolly. That's a tow truck. All skidded up. Look terrible. The man, he got hit and say he walked away but wants his car fixed. How am I gonna get parts? Boss man, he say he know how. I just need to pick up at the dock on Thursday. So here I is. And I sees you boys like you got no wheres to go and nothin to do. So help me with them steel panels and them boxes. I need 'em put on my truck."

Each boy took an end and followed.

"Now look. I wants you two to lay low. You know what that means? Don't be poking your heads into things. Just stay here in the garage. And stay out of the way. You can watch."

At the garage Clarence called himself the chief cook and bottle-washer. He pumped gas, cleaned windshields, checked oil and worked on cars. And just like he said, the Volkswagen looked like a bubble can. The boys were fascinated to see it, which Clarence showed them was completely backwards to any other car.

"Them Germans made it so the engine would push the car, not pull it. If they's so smart, why didn't they win the War? Guess we lucky they didn't."

Much to the boys' surprise and delight, in Baltimore they saw faces often their same hue, sometimes darker, sometimes lighter. But they also saw white faces. In London they were schooled in the proper ways to defer to whites. And because it often brought reward, they took it on faith that deference would help them in the United States. They were also quick imitators and so they sounded quite British with their English.

78

The two boys slept in a corner of the garage. The owner never showed up before nine and always left by five, so to him the boys had simply arrived before him and stayed later. On Clarence's word that they were harmless, the garage owner let them hang around, after all, it was summer.

When September rolled around, Clarence told them they needed to go to school. Nmumba and Yusuf had no formal education and therefore had no idea what to expect. It was September 7, 1954, the first day of school for the two boys and the first day Baltimore public schools opened as racially integrated.

The girls noticed Nmumba. He was tall, broad, dark-skinned and nearly fifteen. Yusuf was thirteen, small and lithe. Clarence had cut their hair and took them clothes shopping. He had started calling them Mike and Little Joe.

"If you want to forget Africa, then you needs to start with new names. I'm calling you Mike." Clarence pointed at Nmumba.

"And you, squirt, I'm calling you Little Joe."

When the boys showed up at school, they didn't know where to go. A teacher pointed them to the main office. A white woman in her fifties looked the boys up and down over her glasses.

"Can I help you?"

"We are here for school," Nmumba announced.

"Which grades are you in?"

"Grades?" Clarence hadn't told them about grades. "What are grades?"

"You know, what grade did you last complete? Tenth? What about you?" She trained her eyes on Yusuf.

"Six," Yusuf said, plucking a number from the air.

79

"Six. So that puts you in seventh this year. Your parents should have received letters telling you which teachers you're assigned to. What did your letters say?"

"We didn't get letters," Nmumba replied.

"Alright then. I will look up your names. Let's start with you." She looked at Nmumba. "Name?"

"Mike. Mike Taylor." He attached Clarence's last name to his new American name.

"And you?" She turned to Yusuf.

"Little Joe—Taylor."

"Let's see what we have for you two." She turned and walked to a file cabinet and pulled open a drawer.

"Well I don't see either of you on our rolls but with this integration thing, I don't know how we're supposed to keep up." She kept thumbing through paper records. "Ruby Taylor—is she related to you?"

"She's our cousin," Yusuf blurted.

"That may explain it. Her parents called and said she was being moved from our school to the other side of town. Maybe you two are meant to—"

"I'm sure we're supposed to be here," Yusuf pleaded, regretting his lie. He did not want to have to walk miles to school.

"I guess the records haven't kept up. Look, boys, you will need to fill out forms. Will you do that for me?" She pulled fresh cards from another drawer, gathered two pencils and laid both on the counter in front of the two. "Just put your name and address and telephone number along with your parents' names. Now, Joe, you say you're in seventh grade? That will be Mrs. Gardner's class. Mike? Which grade are you?"

"Ten."

"Okay. Ten will be Mr. Smith. Just follow the signs. Seventh is Green and Ten is Orange."

The telephone on the secretary's desk rang and she turned to answer it.

Nmumba and Yusuf looked at each other, pocketed the forms and pencils and quietly left.

"How was school?"

Yusuf shrugged. I'm in seventh grade. Everything's green in seventh grade. And they make you eat lunch before everyone else."

"Mike?"

"They didn't know where to put us. You need to sign our cards."

Clarence scowled. "What cards?"

"For the lady in the office." Nmumba reached into his pocket. Yusuf did the same and both handed over their forms.

"We told them our last name was Taylor," Yusuf said.

"Taylor. I see. So you told them you was my boys?"

"Not really. We just said our names were Mike and Joe Taylor."

"I prayed the Lord for sons. Looks like I got 'em."

The boys were not alone in their struggle to read. Mrs. Gardner treated her students with patience and went slowly over assignments. Nmumba's teacher, Mr. Smith was the football coach and didn't much care if his class could read or write. Many days he set up a projector and showed movies like, *The Daily Life of the Wildebeast* and *Appreciating your Parents*. American History meant a discussion of wars requiring memorization of battles and generals. Nmumba made fast friends with the boy beside him who helped him when test-time came. In the evenings, Yusuf and Nmumba retreated to their spot in the garage where they laid out bedrolls from Clarence. During those hours Yusuf tried to teach Nmumba reading and writing.

On Saturdays and late afternoons they worked at the garage. The owner had let Nmumba pick up and empty the trash and sometimes clean and organize the tools the shop. He started paying Nmumba a dollar a day for his work. Yusuf puttered around, often taking a push broom and cleaning the floors and also the toilets, Colored and White.

On Saturday, October 16, 1954 Hurricane Hazel hit Baltimore. Able to read the skies, the boys could tell in advance a serious weather event was brewing.

"We should bring in all the equipment and turn off the pumps," Nmumba warned Clarence.

"What? Are you afraida little rain?"

"This won't be a little rain."

"Suit yourself."

Nmumba and Yufuf dragged items inside the garage including signs and gear, and shut off the gas pumps. That night they hardly slept. Wind whipped fiercely. Yusuf slid closer to his brother. Feeling his warmth reassured him everything would be alright.

At two in the morning a loud roar passed overhead. They heard limbs snap and trees slam to the ground. And then the roar stopped while rain continued to pour.

In the morning, they cautiously opened the garage door. The world beyond was desolate. Roofs were caved in. Trees and powerlines lay on houses, on streets, on each other. The garage building was miraculously spared.

Sirens began wailing.

"What do we do?" Yusuf asked.

"We clean."

At midday Clarence appeared. He walked three miles from his house to the garage.

He hugged the boys to himself. "I was afraid—" He choked back tears. "My house is fine. But look at here." Telephone poles lay scattered and electrical wires dangled everywhere. "I won't doubt you again, Mike, when you tell me a storm is coming. You were smart to turn off them pumps. Has the owner been by?"

"We haven't seen him."

"He probably can't get in. The police have blocked off this area from cars coming through. They don't want people driving over these telephone and powerlines. Look at you boys. You cleaned up the place. I can see the electric's off. Is water still running?"

"Yes. People have been coming over and filling jugs," Nmumba replied.

"Good. Whatever we can do to help."

"Mr. Alexander, we need you to turn this way. Don't look at the camera," a white man in a yellow slicker directed Austin Alexander, a black man in a stylish raincoat. "Look at the reporter, please."

A white reporter for WBAL-TV stood with a microphone in hand. A portable light shined on the pair. A bulky man held an equally large camera on his shoulder.

"We're on in 5, 4, 3, 2..." the director commanded.

"We are in the heart of the City of Baltimore where Hurricane Hazel did its worst damage," the WBAL reporter began. "We have with us Mr. Austin Alexander, the Atlantic regional spokesman for Supreme Property, Casualty and Life Insurance." The camera panned out to include the black man. The reporter continued. "Mr. Alexander, your company is one of the primary insurers of this area. What can you tell us about the processing of claims?" The reporter tipped the mic toward Austin Alexander.

"I would like to assure the people of this neighborhood, of Baltimore City and wherever claims will be filed that Supreme Property, Casualty and Life is eager to help. Our adjusters will be making rounds and taking contact information so claims may be filed and people can begin to rebuild as soon as possible."

"Mr. Alexander, will those who no longer have homes be able to build back what they lost?"

"Policies have various levels of coverage and we will be taking action to provide people with our full attention."

"Will you, yourself be overseeing the process?"

"We have qualified staff who stand ready. And I am rolling up my sleeves to do whatever I can."

"Has your company had to deal with claims of this size before?"

"This may be the largest singular event, but we will do our best to help our policy holders."

"Thank you, Mr. Alexander." The reporter and camera turned their attention to the surrounding block of flattened buildings and area devastation.

"We're out. That's a wrap!" the director shouted.

Mr. Alexander walked over to Clarence who had stayed back from the camera shot. "Is there a place I can wash my hands?"

"Sure thing. Let me show you." Clarence led the well-dressed black man across the cleanly swept garage to the Colored Men's room. He turned on the light and left the man to his business.

When the insurance man stepped out of the restroom he saw Nmumba rolling waste barrels toward him to create an aisle for people now lining up to use the restrooms and to draw water. The neighboring

84

residents had been temporarily halted by the television crew. Now, they were in clusters awaiting access. White and black.

"Water lines affected, too?" Mr. Alexander asked.

"Nmumba nodded. "At least we have water here. No electricity, though." Nmumba thought of Sierra Leone where they didn't have electricity except in large towns. Primitive living came easily to Nmumba who had not taken these commodities for granted. Clean, running water was a luxury.

"Are you from Baltimore?" Mr. Alexander asked.

"No."

"You seem like you are from the old country."

"I am from Africa. Sierra Leone. I have come here to be free. To work and be free."

"Do you work here at this garage?"

"Yes. And I go to school."

"I sometimes need people for special projects. Would you be willing to help me?"

Nmumba didn't answer.

"My family has a history of being on the side of justice for the colored man. I need someone in these Baltimore neighborhoods to develop ties that strengthen our cause. And you can be a symbol of the rise of men recently come to our nation. You have not been spoiled by the polarization and politics we see in every city and neighborhood. You have a kind face. Someone like you can make a difference."

"What do you want me to do?"

"For now, I just want you to keep your ear to the ground. Men come and go from this service station. If you hear things, disturbing things, I want you to telephone me. Here is my business card." Austin Alexander handed Nmumba a white card. It was the first time Nmumba had seen such a thing.

"It has my telephone number for you to call me. The number is our regional headquarters in Washington DC."

Nmumba laughed indicating the downed telephone lines and electrical wires. "It would be easier face-to-face."

"I know. But calling will be better."

Nmumba had been overhearing talk of racial tensions. In school he felt it each day. Mr. Smith wanted Nmumba to play sports. He would have been happy for Nmumba's bulk to block and tackle on the black high school football team. But Nmumba did not like sports. He liked girls. He liked following them and watching them. One girl in particular had caught his eye, Regina. Her skin was coffee and cream colored, smooth as silk. Her eyes playfully met his then darted away. He knew she liked him, but he did not know how to approach her. She was always surrounded by other girls.

"Nmumba, I heard today that the students want to cause trouble," Yusuf said. The boys were walking to the garage after school. "The whites think they don't get what they should, that we are holding them back. They say they will boycott school."

"It's just talk, Yusuf. The whites want to play god. They think they are better. Don't listen to them."

"I think it's real. And some people think they will burn down houses of black people."

"Burn their houses?"

"That's what I heard."

"That sounds like talk to me."

"Wait and see, Nmumba. Just wait and see."

~~~

A reporter stood across from the school. A WBAL-TV truck sat nearby. A cluster of white newsmen stood around it smoking. Another man balanced a large camera on his shoulder as a reporter spoke.

"Five people died in a house fire in Baltimore City last night. Fireman are investigating the cause, believing it was purposely set. The house is in the neighborhood of Calhoun High School which has been integrated since the Brown versus Board of Education ruling last year."

"I told you," Yusuf mumbled to Nmumba as they walked into school.

After school Nmumba found Austin Alexander's business card. He had never actually placed a telephone call, but he had watched many others drop a dime in the machine and talk into the receiver. He fished a dime from his pocket, and looking to be sure no one was watching, he strolled to the pay telephone on the side of the lot.

"Please deposit one dollar and forty-five cents," a voice said when he dialed the number. He thought it was only a dime. He hung up the phone, confused. He went to his corner of the garage to his stash of cash and counted out coins. He returned to the pay phone, dropped in the dime, dialed and this time when the voice told him how much to deposit, he did. The coins sounded funny falling into the machine.

"Supreme Property, Casualty and Life," a woman's voice answered.

"Can I talk to Mr. Alexander?"

"Just one moment," the voice chirped.

"Austin Alexander."

"Mr. Alexander, this is Nmumba—I mean Mike Taylor. I met you after the hurricane in Baltimore. You gave me your phone number."

"Yes, the young man from Sierra Leone. What can I do for you?"

87

"You told me to call you if something seemed strange or bad for blacks. I think people are setting fire to houses around our school. My brother says his friends heard white boys saying they were going to burn down houses. One has already been destroyed. Five people died."

"I saw that. You believe it was school kids?"

"I don't know. I'm just telling you what my brother told me."

"Can you find out more? Are you friends with anyone who would know?"

"Not really. We don't mix. But I will ask my brother."

"If he knows anything, please call me again. This is very helpful. Thank you, Mike."

"Roger was bragging to Billy. I overheard him talking. He didn't know I was there," Yusuf said.

"What did Roger say?" Nmumba asked.

"He said, `It serves them right for trying to take over our school. We have to fight for what is ours. They are trying to take it away and we can't stand back and let them do it.'"

"Is Billy with him?"

"I think Roger was trying to get him to join him."

"Did he say if they were going to set more fires or do anything else?"

"I couldn't hear after that."

"You could play football. Why don't you? Are you scared you might get hurt, Mikey?" Roger taunted Nmumba. He had come over to the colored row in the locker room after showering and snapped his towel toward Nmumba.

Nmumba just stared.

"You think you can beat us. You can't. We have been here longer than you. And we know a thing or two. You are a scourge. I bet you don't even know what that is. Scourge rhymes with turd. That's what you are—a turd scourge." He laughed and retreated to his all-white row in the room.

"Roger is the devil. He is planning something," Nmumba whispered.

"What can we do? Should we tell the Principal?" Regina asked, looking intently at Nmumba. The two were working at the last table at the back of their Chemistry classroom. Nmumba was pleased they were lab partners.

"Will the Principal believe *us*? He is white. We are black," Nmumba said.

"Roger likes to think he's a big man, but his father only works on the railroad. His little brother Tommy isn't bad. I think he's in your brother's grade. Maybe Joe can find out something by talking to him," Regina said.

"How would Joe talk to Tommy?"

"I don't know. Say something about school, maybe?"

"You know as well as I do how hard it is to talk to white people in this school."

"I bet your brother could if he tried."

"Hey, Tommy. Wait up!" Yusuf called to the boy on the sidewalk. Running to catch up, Yusuf met the white boy who had paused in place. "I want to ask you about our geography homework. I didn't write it down."

"Read chapters twenty and twenty-one. We have a quiz tomorrow."

"I know, that's why I wanted to know." Yusuf paused to catch his breath. "Do you like geography?"

"I guess. It's interesting. But I like English Lit more."

"Me, too. Mrs. Gardner says we can put on a play at the end of the year. Which one do you think she will choose?" Yusuf asked.

89

"*A Winter's Tale*. She likes that one."

"I like when she does the different voices. She could be an actress."

Yusuf tossed his books onto the sidewalk and suddenly assumed an actor's pose. He threw out his arms gesturing toward Tommy.

"'How say you? My prisoner or my guest? One of them you shall be!'"

Tommy play acted, too. "'We knew not the doctrine of ill-doing, nor dreamed that any did.'"

Yusuf bent on one knee and gazed up at Tommy. "'We were as twinned lambs that did frisk in the sun. And did bleat the one at the other. What we exchanged was innocence for innocence.'"

Tommy stared down at Yusuf who looked up with folded hands held at his heart.

Then Tommy began, "'Press me not, beseech you, so. There is no tongue that moves, none, none in the world, so soon as yours could win me. My affairs do drag me homeward, which to hinder were in your love a whip to me; my stay to you a charge and trouble, to save both. Farewell, our brother.'" Tommy appeared truly pained.

Yusuf stood up and they looked at each other. Their synergetic energy could have sparked a fire.

The moment faded. Yusuf picked up his books and Tommy turned to resume walking.

"Hey, we could read one of the plays together sometime. Would you like to?" Yusuf walked with Tommy, stride for stride.

"Sure," Tommy said, a tinge of delight in his voice.

"You choose."

"*The Importance of Being Earnest*," Tommy announced, then took off running toward home.

90

~~~

The boys were in a room at school where props had been stored. Each had dragged in a chair. Tommy shut the door. "We won't be seen here," Tommy said.

"What do you like about *The Importance of Being Earnest?*"

"It's funny. It has all these plot twists. And it's fun to dress up. You can be Jack. I will be Algernon. We can take turns with the other characters."

They began reading, levity and laughter lacing their hour. Yusuf was delighted to be able to read aloud. When he stumbled, Tommy rescued him without recrimination. Yusuf delivered his final line with flourish.

"On the contrary, Aunt Augusta, I've now realized for the first time in my life the vital importance of being Earnest."

Tommy sat with his hands in his lap, looking down.

"What's wrong? I thought you liked this play?"

"I do. It's my favorite. No one else likes plays."

"I do."

Tommy sighed.

"You mean none of your white friends?"

Tommy jerked up his script and started to put it in his bag.

"I don't mind, Tommy."

Tommy stopped and turned to face Yusuf. "Joe, you don't know, do you?"

"Know what?"

"We can't be friends. If we're seen together it will mean…"

"Will mean what?"

"Look, my family, my brother, my father. They don't understand. They think colored people are trying to take over the world, or at least our country. They feel they have the right to defend it. I'm sorry."

91

"Do you feel that way?" Yusuf's heart pounded as he asked this.

"No. No, I don't. I think that my dad gets stuff in his head and starts to believe it. Probably doesn't help that he works on the railroad."

"Why? What's bad about the railroad?"

"Those men are brutal. They say things they think are funny. But really, they are mean. Very mean."

"I knew men like that in Falaba."

"Where is Falaba?"

"In Sierra Leone, where I'm from."

"So you really are from Africa? How do you speak such good English?"

"I learned. I was in England for a while, too."

"England?"

"In London."

"That explains the way you talk. What does your father do?"

Yusuf hesitated. "He mines for diamonds."

"Diamonds? Has he ever found any?"

"Sure." Yusuf stopped short of saying anything else.

"When you leave today, don't go the way you always go."

"Why?"

"Look, it's just not good for you to go that way."

"How do you know?"

"I heard my brother talking to his friends yesterday. They are planning another *lesson* he called it."

Yusuf's eyes widened. "Another fire?"

"Don't tell anyone."

"But people could die."

"Roger said they won't risk more deaths. They're just destroying houses. They are scared they will still be caught for the last fire. Roger knows it's wrong, but he feels justified. Like he's a soldier in a war. He used to try to get me to play war with him. I never understood the point."

Yusuf felt sick.

"Why didn't you tell me they were going to set another house on fire?" Nmumba demanded.

Yusuf was silent.

"You knew, didn't you?"

Yusuf turned and went into the garage.

Clarence called over. "Hey Little Joe. I need you to clean them bathrooms. Bossman say they needs paper, too."

Nmumba walked over to Yusuf who was dropping his school books in their corner. He pulled his younger brother around toward him.

"Why didn't you tell me?"

"I couldn't. I promised I wouldn't tell."

"Promised who? Promised who?"

Yusuf said nothing.

"Tommy told you, didn't he? I need to let Mr. Alexander know when this is going to happen. He has people who can stop it."

"You think so?"

"I know so. You *must* tell me when Roger is going to do this again. We have to stop them."

"At least no one was hurt."

"No one was hurt?! What about their house? Their belongings?"

The boys often conversed in their native tongue when they didn't want Clarence to understand them.

"Hey, you boys. Stop talking Africano and get to work."

Yusuf and Tommy placed scripts into their book bags. They were in the prop room finishing another play. Tommy paused and turned to Yusuf.

93

"They're planning another *lesson* for tonight."

"Where?" Yusuf tried to sound casual.

"You know the old Negro lady that yells at them when they toss trash in her yard? They said they've had enough of her. I don't know if they plan to do it while she's there or not. Seems like she never leaves."

"Tommy, we can't let her die in her house."

"I know."

"I think I know someone who can help."

"Who?"

"The insurance man who was on television after the hurricane. He is trying to stop things like this."

"I can't get my brother arrested."

"Would you rather an old lady die?"

Nmumba shoved change into the pay telephone at the garage.

"Austin Alexander."

"Mr. Alexander, this is Mike Taylor. I have a tip that a third fire is to be set over here tonight."

"Where?"

Nmumba gave him the address.

"How certain are you?"

"One hundred percent."

"Thank you."

Black men dressed in black clothes stepped out of the shadows with baseball bats. One swung his and connected with a white boy's torso. Another used his bat to hit a different white boy in the gut. A third white boy was clubbed from behind with a bat to his knees. He buckled and fell. The black men slipped away as quietly as they had arrived, leaving three white boys lying on the ground.

94

~~~

"How did they know?" Tommy' father's voice rose in volume and urgency. "How did they know?" He grabbed his son by the hair.

"I don't know." Tommy cowered.

"You *do* know." Tommy's father raised his hand and smacked the boy in the head. You heard your brother and then told on him. You were with that nigger again, weren't you?"

Tommy gasped, his eyes wide.

"You think I don't know. You and that colored getting into your famous dress up parties. You fruit. You're a goddamned fruit! And what's worse, with a nigger!" He smashed his fists into his son's body.

"No, Dad, please! No!"

"Men, we have us a job to do. Let's go hunt us some nigger tonight."

Four white men drove over to the garage in the dark. The garage door was closed and Nmumba and Yusuf both would have been in bed but Yusuf was in the bathroom when the men broke in. Their faces covered, they carried torches and started swinging them around in search of the young boy.

Nmumba hearing them sat up. Realizing his mistake he immediately lay back but it was too late.

"Over here!" One of the men shouted.

The men pulled back the covers and stuck a torch at Nmumba's face.

"You little snot-nosed nigger. You're coming with us."

But Nmumba was not little. Nmumba kicked and bucked when the men grabbed him. He tried to make himself heavy but the men were able to drag him from his bed and splay him on the floor. One of the men tramped on Nmumba's head to keep him in place. Then, the men

95

tied Nmumba's hands behind his back, yanked him up by the hair and marched him to their waiting truck.

Behind the bathroom door Yusuf, petrified, shook uncontrollably. They had come for him and had taken his brother. Why hadn't he come out and tried to save Nmumba? But he would only have been hauled away, too. Was this Tommy's father's gang of men? How did they know it was he who had tipped off Roger's plan? He shook so hard he couldn't think what to do. He knew where Clarence lived. He would run there.

"Whoo Hoo. We got us a live one! Looky here," one of the white men called as he yanked Nmumba from the back of his truck where he had been forced to lie.

The men drove more than an hour south of the city to an open field. A huge bonfire burned as the four men shoved Nmumba into a circle of other men covered in white sheets with white hats shaped like cones. The men began to chant eerily. Nmumba was terrified. His hands remained bound behind him. The man with the truck pushed Nmumba onto his knees. One by one each white man came into the circle, spit on Nmumba and kicked him. When Nmumba wailed, one of them stuffed a rag in his mouth. Another man brought out a baseball bat. Another unsheathed a knife. The fire blazed. The chanting continued. Nmumba fainted from terror and pain.

"They've taken Nmumba!"

"Who?"

"We've got to do something!" Yusuf could hardly get out words. As he talked he tugged at Clarence to follow him.

Clarence took the boy by the shoulders to calm him. "Catch you breath. You about to pop. Now start at the top."

"Men broke into the garage. They were looking for me. They took Nmumba. They took him away."

"Were they white?"

"I think so. I was in the bathroom."

"Where they take him?"

"I don't know."

"Were they driving?"

"Yes, I heard trucks. Pickup trucks."

"What direction they go?"

"I couldn't tell."

"How long ago?"

"I ran right here."

"Well, that would be fifteen minutes, at least. Theys could be anywhere."

Clarence came outside. He let the storm door slam and motioned for Yusuf to sit with him on his front steps.

The two sat in silence.

"I think we should call the insurance man," Yusuf said.

"What insurance man?"

"You remember. The man who was on television after the hurricane. He gave Nmumba his phone number. Nmumba called him when he found out about the fire."

"Which fire?" Clarence scowled. "Are you boys mixed up in that?"

"My friend Tommy knew that another fire was going to be set. So I told Nmunba and he called the insurance man."

"What the insurance man got to do with this?"

"He said he has ways to deal with this."

"I guess he worried that black folk are being burned out and his company got to pay."

"He's a good man—I think. I need to find his telephone number. Then we can call and ask him to help us find Nmumba. Can we go back to the garage?"

Clarence nodded. "Git in my truck."

"Here. Here's the telephone number." Yusuf produced the business card and handed it to Clarence. "Can you call?"

"I don't believe the man is going to answer tonight. This his bidness number."

"Can we drive around and look for Nmumba?" Yusuf strained to do something. Just seeing the place where his brother had been made him desperately sick and afraid.

"I don't think so. They could be anywhere. Best we can do is pray."

Yusuf collapsed into Clarence who held him close.

"You come home with me. Git you kit. And you brother's."

Yusuf did as he was told. His life was all about carrying. And now he would carry everything precious in the world, his brother's belongings.

"May I speak with Mr. Alexander, please?"

"Who's calling, please?"

"He won't know me. Name's Taylor, Clarence Taylor. Tell him I'm— tell him I'm the father of Mike Taylor, from the filling station in Balmor."

"Just one moment, sir."

Austin Alexander came onto the line. "Mr. Taylor. Thank you for calling me. What can I do for you?"

"Little Joe say that men took Mike away last night."

"Any idea where?"

"Yous and I know it wadn't to no candy store."

Austin Alexander paused. "I will see what I can find out. Do you have any information at all? How many men? What they looked like?"

"The boy said it was probably three or four. He never saw 'em. He was in the bathroom. He say they were comin for him, not Mike."

"Why would they be coming for him?"

"Because he squealed on the boys who were planning to set the next fire. Did you know about that Mr. Alexander?"

"I never meant for the boys to get hurt. They came to get Joe but they took Mike instead?"

"That's right."

"You better keep Joe laid low. They may want him, too."

"Can you explain this to me?"

But Austin Alexander had already hung up.

"How about you stay home from school today?"

Yusuf shot Clarence a look. "Why?"

"You don't want to mix yourself up in this more than you are. You can come with me to the garage, but you lay low."

Whenever a car pulled in and ran over the trip cord for the bell to sound, Clarence would trot out from the garage, tip his hat and ask how he could serve the customer. It wasn't long before word came in from one of these customers that three white high school boys were beaten by black men with clubs a few blocks away. Clarence couldn't help but notice that none of today's customers were white.

When Yusuf appeared Clarence waved him off and ordered him back into the garage.

Yusuf could hardly believe the nightmare of missing his brother. He wanted reassurance that Nmumba was all right. That everything would be all right. They had been across oceans together, lived in different countries, survived even when they didn't know the language. And now to come to America to be free only to be separated and—he stopped himself from imagining. In agony, he paced through the garage trying to focus but grief veiled his vision.

The day wore on forever. When it was finally time to close up Clarence came over to Yusuf who was sitting sobbing in his corner.

"Now look, little Joe. You gonna stay with me long as necessary. My rooms need paint and you can be the one to do it. Tomorrow I will git our supplies and show you how it's done."

The next day was Saturday, which was still a work day, but the garage closed early which allowed Clarence time to pick up paint, rollers, brushes and supplies. He used his last pocket money for this one good cause.

"Put 'em here," Clarence said, indicating his table.

Clarence's house was a simple place with no real yard. He was bordered by other houses tight up against his. The inside he kept reasonably neat, with a sofa and two living room chairs. The table had four chairs and a buffet. The two bedrooms each had a bed, and the house had one bathroom.

"The whole house need a fresh coat of paint. I got here India blue. Pretty, don't you think?"

Yusuf shrugged.

"We go room by room. Let's start with the living room. We move everything into the middle, lay an old sheet over it, cover the floor and then start to work."

"Mr. Taylor?" a timid voice called.

Clarence rolled out from under a car and looked up to see a white boy about Yusuf's age. "You need me?" Clarence asked.

"Mr. Taylor. I'm Tommy, Joe's—friend." Tommy hesitated not knowing what to call himself, white and black friendships being so uncommon. "Is he okay? I haven't seen him in school."

"Why you ask?" Clarence gave the boy a skeptical glare and stood up, towering over the boy.

"I hear that Mike hasn't been to school, either. Are they okay?"

"What do you know about this fire bidniss?" Clarence asked. He rubbed his hands with a shop towel.

Tommy hung his head. Clarence could see bruises by the boy's ear and a swollen spot on his head. "You one of them?"

"No."

Clarence kept rubbing his hands with the towel. He looked the boy in the eye. "You knows Mike was taken."

"No! Who? When?"

"Some folks broke into here the other night and took Mike away. No sign since."

Tommy looked frightened.

"Is Joe okay?"

"He stayin with me."

Tommy nodded. "Would you give him this?" Tommy held a book. "What this?"

"The script for the school play. If he wants to try out."

"I don't think he be—"

"Please, just give it to him. It will mean a lot."

"Lay it over there, my hands' dirty." Clarence indicated the work bench. The boy did as he was told then turned to Clarence.

"Can you tell him that I—I—miss him?" Tommy said, then turned and ran.

"Did you call Mr. Alexander? What did he say?" Yusuf asked Clarence.

101

"He say he look into it. I called the police, too, but they won't do nothing."

"It's been four days. We have to do something."

"Keep paintin, Little Joe. Keep paintin."

"Mr. Alexander. This is Mr. Taylor again. We hasn't seen the boy Mike in six days now. We's worried sick."

"I have been looking into the situation, Mr. Taylor. I wish I had better news." Austin Alexander paused and took a deep breath. "I'm afraid all signs point to a lynching."

"I suspect. What do we do about it?"

"Did you report Mike missing to the police?"

"They no help. The boy wasn't a registered citizen. They feel they have no need to look into it. Just another annoying Negro. They make excuses. This is Balmor, 1954. You think they realize we ain't going away. They need to treat us like we all citizens," Clarence said.

"I can tell you that if we come up with any evidence, we will press charges."

"You best believe it. Little Joe and me, we sick over it. Terrible, terrible sick. I did what you said. I keep him away from school. I don't like him being around them whites. They stirrin up trouble of all kinds."

"I guess you can keep him out, but I don't think whoever's responsible will still come for him. They did their damage."

"He's livin with me, at least temporary. I have him paintin the house. Give him something to do. A goal, a focus other than his brother."

"Then let him go back to school so he can get in a routine again."

"If you say."

"Mr. Taylor? I am sorry about all this."

"You didn't do this."

Austin Alexander hesitated.

"I'm glad he has you. I'm glad he has you, Mr. Taylor," the insurance man repeated.

"I's glad to have him."

"Do you think you would adopt him?"

"Me? Adopt? I don't know how any a that's done."

"If I were able to help you file the papers and, say, cover the costs?"

"Well, I never considered it."

"It would put him on better footing. He has no rights at all, now. What little he could have, he should have. And mark my words, Mr. Taylor, the day will come when the black man will rise to power. If we can help one another, we should."

"Amen to that."

15

WASHINGTON SPRING

"We can be like the Mod Squad. I'll be Linc," Jimmy announced. "I always did like Linc's hair. And you be Julie." Jimmy pointed to Mary Gray. "That leaves you to be Pete, Loverboy." Jimmy indicated Bryan.

"Won't we be more like Rodgers and Hammerstein?" Mary Gray asked.

"Jennens and Handel," Bryan said.

"Well, whoever. Let's just do it!"

Mary Gray was sitting cross-legged on Bryan and Jimmy's persimmon-colored sofa drinking champagne. She was not one to drink, but her neighbors had talked her into helping them celebrate their anniversary. Bryan had a soda while Jimmy and Mary Gray shared the champagne. The two were more than a little tipsy.

"I think it's a wonderful idea!" Mary Gray exclaimed. "We'll call the musical *Middle-Aged Madness*."

"That's perfect. We all go a little crazy at this stage of life," Jimmy said, holding up his glass.

"Mostly from lack of sleep. Really. Don't you think most of it is due to lack of sleep?" Mary Gray slurred.

"I haven't had a full night's sleep so far this century," mumbled Bryan.

"I know! We can substitute the words in popular songs that our generation would know. *I could have danced all night* becomes *Wish I could've slept all night, wish I could've slept all night. I still could sleep some more…*" Mary Gray sang.

"That's funny, Mary Gray," Bryan said.

"How about Sting's *Every little thing she does is magic*. We could make that, *Every little thing he does is maddening. Everything he does just turns me off*? Jimmy added.

"Whoo hoo! This is great!" Mary Gray got up and started circling the cottage looking for pen and paper. "Where do you two keep a note-pad?" She wobbled a little. Then giggled. She hadn't had this much fun since summer camp.

Sober Bryan took charge. "I'll lay out the show. You two come up with the songs."

"Mary Gray? We have us a job to do." Jimmy laughed as he turned over the bottle for the last few drops.

Angelika sat at her desk and chewed on a pen cap. She had completed the closing paperwork of her aunt's estate and had made her last trip to the lawyer's office. What gnawed at her was the attorney's report. The money from the sale of her aunt's house had covered her Washington Spring entry fee. And the estate's remaining assets should have been enough to carry her through to the end of her earthly days. What she had not known was that the estate would have to pay substantial tax to the state of Maryland. The attorney had withheld this critical inform-ation yet he had not withheld his large, now paid to himself, bill. The attorney did not explain that to come up with the tax money he would have to liquidate a substantial portion of her aunt's remaining stocks and bonds.

Her decision to buy into Washington Spring now seemed not only impractical but also untenable. She and her son were quite literally broke.

16

BALTIMORE
1960

"You got Valedictorian, Tommy. I knew you would," exclaimed Yusuf.

"I don't know why."

"Yes, you do. You are an A student and teachers like you. You're the smartest person in our class, probably our whole school." Yusuf sounded enthusiastic and wistful.

"That's just because I can remember stuff. I have one of those memories. But you do, too. Look at the lines you knew for the school play. You were a great help to me getting ready for *Our Town*. I couldn't have done it without you. But, Joe, you should've had the lead."

"Sure, a black kid getting to play George Gibbs. Besides, you're going to Juilliard."

"You know what I mean. You're a better actor than me. I wish you were coming with me. I wish you would've applied."

"I heard from Howard University."

"And?"

"I got in."

"See, I told you that you could do it!"

The boys eagerly embraced.

17

WASHINGTON SPRING

"Come in Mary Gray." Bryan made a show of welcoming his neighbor and co-writer into their writing hovel also known as Bryan and Jimmy's cottage.

"We've got news!" Jimmy chirped. "Better sit down, Mary Gray."

She took a seat in the living room on the persimmon-colored sofa.

"*Middle-Aged Madness* has a buyer in Baltimore. A theatre there wants to put it on."

"You can't be serious, Bryan. You submitted our show to a theatre in Baltimore? I didn't know you even knew anyone in the theatre." Mary Gray gaped at Bryan.

"There's a lot about my partner you don't know," Jimmy said, winking conspiratorially. Jimmy perched himself on the arm of the sofa and smiled slyly.

"He's an old music conservatory friend who works for the Worthington Theatre of Performing Arts," Bryan said. "Worthington does classics and new works. He said they especially like musicals. So I took the liberty of forwarding him a draft of *Middle-Aged Madness*."

"And?"

"He loves it. I'll be talking to him tomorrow."

"If Worthington Theatre wants to do the show what would that mean?" Mary Gray looked earnestly at Bryan.

"If we're lucky I guess we'll find out."

Mary Gray glanced at her watch. She had thirty minutes to get to the county library before they closed. She had reserved several Parabar County history chronicles and one how-to book on getting a script from paper to the stage. She pulled on her coat, picked up her purse and keys and started out the door. Just then her cell phone rang. When she saw it was Bryan she answered.

"Hi Bryan," she said while walking toward her car, keys at the ready.

"Worthington Theatre wants to put on *Middle-Aged Madness*," Bryan announced.

"You're joking." Mary Gray stopped walking.

"I'm not. Why else have we been meeting every Monday, Wednesday and Friday for these many months to work on this thing?"

"I know, but I thought we were doing it for fun," Mary Gray said.

"And for the love of money." Jimmy shouted in the background. "I want my third of the spoils," he declared.

"How does this even work? Do we sell the rights? Do we get a cut of the ticket sales?" Mary Gray asked.

"We sell the script. The producers put up the money and take the risk. And therefore get the rewards."

"What would a script like ours sell for?"

110

"If this were Broadway, maybe ten thousand dollars."

"That's all?" Jimmy complained. Mary Gray could hear Jimmy in the background. "When you think about what the big shows take in, that's nothing, and we're the ones who wrote it!" Jimmy continued.

"Well this isn't Broadway, so temper your dreams, Jimmy. First, let's see if we can work out a deal. Mary Gray, I wanted to let you know."

"I'm on my way to the library," she continued walking to her car, "to pick up a book on producing stage plays. Maybe it will be useful."

"You're the researcher, Mary Gray. We'll be happy for whatever you find. Let's rendezvous on Wednesday as usual. We can compare notes then."

Mary Gray sat down with Bryan and Jimmy at their dining room table where the three did their composing. During the trio's first efforts at serious writing, Bryan had slid his music keyboard close to the table so he could play the familiar songs while Mary Gray and Jimmy tested their new lyrics. Today there were no scores. No drafts. No keyboard. It was just the three of them.

"So you're saying that your conservatory friend suddenly decided to retire and now he doesn't want to do our show?" Jimmy fussed.

"It may be a blessing."

"How can it be a blessing?" Jimmy demanded.

"He wants *Middle-Aged Madness* for Worthington Theatre believe me, but apparently the board of directors is basically forcing him out. They came to him with a `recommendation.'" Bryan's fingers formed air quotes. "The upshot is, he wants me to talk with a producer friend of his."

"At Worthington?"

"No. On Broadway."

111

"Broadway?! What happened to Worthington?" Mary Gray exclaimed.

"Let's just say that my friend is well-connected. He also feels no lingering loyalty to the new board president and would like to see us succeed. He's preparing an introduction for us."

"On Broadway." Mary Gray took that in. "What's the man's name?"

"Thomas Kittering, a longstanding Broadway producer."

"For real?" Mary Gray asked.

"For real. And if I know my friend, he will make this count."

"Is this Bryan Beal?"

"Yes, speaking."

"This is Thomas Kittering. How are you?"

"Fine, thank you. How are you?"

"Never better. I'll come to the point. I've read *Middle-Aged Madness* and my partner and I would like to make an offer for your script. It's quirky. It's funny. It will appeal to the type of audience that still goes to the theatre, namely people our age. I trust you are this same age?"

"Sixty-seven."

"I made seventy-seven last week. You'd think I'd quit this racket. Our music school friend has sense enough to get out while he can, his reputation intact. I seem to keep taking chances. And I would like your script to be my last voyage. It seems appropriate enough."

"I'm flattered, thank you."

"My partner and I want to come up with a respectable offer. I just want to know if you've shopped this to anyone else?"

"No, we haven't." Bryan wondered if he should have said, *not yet*.

"Good. My partner and I will talk and I will get back in contact within forty-eight hours. Will that be enough time to keep you from sending the script out to others?"

"We can agree to that."

"I promise you I will be back in touch."

Bryan telephoned Mary Gray.

"I think the Broadway producer really likes the script. He says he will call again in two days with an offer."

"How will we know if it's fair?"

"I've been reading that book you got from the library. I have a feeling the offer will be solid. And if it's not, I will know what to do."

18

WASHINGTON SPRING

"Leena! Great to hear from you. Let me get Natalie." Ben called Natalie over to the phone. He pressed the speaker button. "Okay. We've got you now, Leena."

"It turns out the bones are from a teen male. Forensics analyzed the jaw and other bones and could tell that much. And that his jaw bone showed severe trauma like he had been hit there. I understand that's not much to go on. The bones are quite deteriorated and soft. If you could do some research on African Americans who died in Parabar County from 1950 through 1970 you may come up with something."

"We know just the person for the job," Ben said.

"Mary Gray?"

"Ben how are you?" Mary Gray rested the phone on her shoulder so she could continue ironing altar cloths for St. James.

114

"Natalie and I need to ask a favor. Last fall we were out mushroom hunting not far from Washington Spring, the real Washington Spring, you know, that little waterway George Washington used to keep his men and horses alive? Natalie and I were looking for mushrooms when we stumbled onto some old bones that were actually human remains. Our anthropologist friend, Leena Chandler took them to her lab up at Cornell and was able to establish that they were from a teenage African American male. However, that's all she could say, and that he was buried at least fifty years ago. Leena suspects foul play since there was no grave marker and his jaw bone indicates a severe blow. She suggests researching county records for African Americans in Parabar County who died between 1950 and 1970. Would you know how to do that?"

"I should be able to. When do you need to know?"

"He's been dead a long time, but it would be nice to solve this mystery as soon as possible."

"I'll see what I can find."

"Bryan? This is Thomas Kittering. Thank you for your patience. My partner and I would like to offer you $10,000 for *Middle-Aged Madness*."

Bryan was prepared. "We would like to accept your offer but we feel it could be worth more."

"This is your first script, I believe? What do you propose?"

"Twenty."

"How about fifteen?"

"I believe my co-writers can accept that."

"Alright then. Now. We need some changes."

"Changes?"

"The script needs editing."

"I see." Bryan moved the phone from one shoulder to the other.

"Mr. Beal, that *is* how it goes in the business. Look, it's a solid musical. We really like it. Overall it works. We just have some parts that need to be re-written. Will your group have trouble with that?"

"I'm sure we can handle it," Bryan agreed. He doodled on a tablet.

"How far are you from Baltimore? We have to be in Baltimore to close up a family estate. If you're not far, my partner and I could meet in person and get the revised script from you."

"We're an hour, depending on traffic."

"Good. I'll send you our notes on the needed edits. Then the middle of next month we'll drive on down to you and see what you have. That gives you three weeks for the revisions."

"I'm sure that will work," Bryan declared, not sure if it actually would.

A week later Mary Gray knocked on the door of Ben and Natalie's cottage.

"Come in, Mary Gray," Ben said, opening the door wide.

Their same 1,100 square feet was outfitted in gold and green with traditional furnishings. She took a seat in the living room placing her notepad on her lap.

"Hi Mary Gray," Natalie said, joining them.

"I did the research you asked. From the county records, there were remarkably few African American people living in Parabar County from 1950 to 1970, and those who died during those years all appear to be accounted for. I didn't find any missing persons reports. Since there was no grave marker, I would say that whoever buried this man did not want his grave found. Nothing of what you told me matches anything in Parabar County. That leads me to wonder if the young man was killed elsewhere and brought into the county."

"How will we know?" Natalie asked.

"Mary Gray shrugged. "The sad truth is during that time vigilante groups still took their form of justice into their own hands. This man may have been lynched."

"Oh my god," Natalie exclaimed.

The three were quiet.

"We should have a proper burial," Ben said.

"See if your friend can return the bones to you." Mary Gray said.

"Yes. I will do that," Ben said.

"Mr. Barclay? This is Mary Gray Walterson. You remember our visit last winter?" Mary Gray held the phone close to her ear.

"Why yes, and a pleasant one it was. What can I do for you?"

"You may be able to help me with some research I'm doing."

"Oh? What kind of research?"

"I would prefer to talk about it in person."

"Well, that sounds mysterious. I suppose you could come any time. When would suit you?"

"How about tomorrow afternoon at two o'clock?"

"That's fine. I look forward to seeing you again. The last time you asked about my Barclay ancestors. I hope I can provide you with what you need this time."

"I hope so, too."

Richard Barclay's home was just as Mary Gray remembered, a stone house from two centuries earlier with more recent additions to accommodate a modern family. She could hear his beagles baying in the backyard pen. She knocked on the front door.

"Ms. Walterson!" Richard Barclay exclaimed as he opened the door. "So nice to see you again." He waved her inside. His bushy gray eyebrows framed brilliant blue eyes. His body had compressed with age giving him a bow-legged appearance.

"Thank you, Mr. Barclay. I am flattered you remembered me."

"It's not so often I get visitors and I relish each one with delight. Please come in."

He ushered her into the living room. Newspapers and magazines were in neat stacks rather than scattered across the furnishings as they had been on her first visit.

"What may I offer you to drink? Hot tea? Cold tea? Or do you prefer coffee?"

"Hot tea would be lovely."

"I'll just be a minute."

Five minutes later Richard Barclay emerged with a tray holding china tea cups and saucers, a small milk pitcher and sugar bowl. "Now, let me offer you a choice."

"Black is fine, thank you."

"I enjoy my tea with milk and sugar. Puts a smile on my face."

The two settled in, tea cups balanced on their laps.

"Now, you have something you think I can help with?"

"I have some delicate questions you may be able to answer." She took a breath. "Some bones turned up not far from here."

"Bones? Animal bones?"

"Human bones."

"Oh. I was going to say, we've buried our dogs through the years. But human bones. What do you make of them?"

"Forensic analysis indicates the bones are fifty or more years old from a teenaged male of African descent."

"Go on."

"There are surprisingly few African Americans registered in Parabar County between 1950 and 1970, the time frame of these remains."

Richard was silent.

"There was no marker or gravestone to indicate a standard burial."

"Sounds like someone didn't care to mark the grave or perhaps it's been lost."

"Forensic analysis also indicates the individual may have had a blow to the jaw."

Mary Gray tried to sound casual as if they were discussing the weather. She was well-aware she was sitting with a landholder spanning many generations who might not take kindly to her questions.

He said nothing.

She sipped her tea allowing her words to sink in.

Richard Barclay sighed and then he began.

"I saw a terrible thing once, a long time ago. I was sixteen." His words came out slowly. His eyes remained on his tea.

"I heard such a ruckus from my daddy's dogs. They knew someone was on our land. They could hear and smell the way dogs can. My father wasn't home so I thought I better check what was going on. I don't know why I felt so brave. I didn't even take one of the dogs with me. I guess I didn't yet know the extent of evil in the world." Richard Barclay looked up scarcely meeting Mary Gray's eyes.

"It was night. Outside I could smell smoke so I started walking that way. At first I thought maybe the woods were on fire, maybe I should call the fire company. But a little farther on I heard a sound I will never forget as long as I live. Someone was pounding on a drum and men were chanting like moaning demons. I crept along until I came close enough to see." He hesitated and looked down again at his tea.

"I watched twenty men beat, cut and club a black man to death. I thought they would hang him but I think he died before they could do that. Two men were digging a grave. When they threw in the body they each took turns urinating and one even defecated on the body. At least

119

that's what it looked like to me. I didn't want to see any more, so as silently as I could I got myself back to the house. I didn't know what to do. I knew the sheriff would be too late to do anything."

Richard Barclay set his cup and saucer on a nearby table. With his hands free, he folded them in his lap.

"The next day I went to the spot and except for evidence of the bonfire and some overturned soil, nothing looked different than normal. The man they killed was dead and I couldn't bring him back to life. So, I guess I've just lived with it all these years." He paused, unable to meet Mary Gray's eyes.

Now he glanced her way. Her eyes held his but he couldn't be sure if it was to convey guilt or understanding.

In a fresh voice he resumed the story. "My boys believe this place is haunted. When they were young I chalked it up to their fantastic imaginations. But one time they told me about a black boy who came to them in the woods. They were sleeping outside. This was before they started with this haunting business. They were camped out a summer night and they said a black teenager appeared to them asking how to get to Baltimore. They said he was wearing odd clothes and had a faraway look in his eyes. My boys weren't driving yet so they could only point in a general direction. They said the black boy turned and walked back into the woods. I didn't think much of it until I started to really consider what they had said. We hadn't had a colored family in Parabar Shore. And I couldn't imagine where this black boy had come from. And then one day my mind went to that god-awful night in 1954. I didn't say anything to my boys. I didn't want to frighten them. But then they told me they saw him again. They were out hunting squirrels with their BB guns. And they said the same teenager showed up again asking for directions to Baltimore. The boys said there was something not right about him. They thought maybe he was retarded. But once again he

120

drifted off. I believe my oldest started to realize this wasn't a human person, I mean an alive person, but a spirit. And that's when they started with the haunting stories. I had a hard time convincing them they were imagining too much. They liked to read those Hardy Boys books, so I tried to pass it off like they were too wrapped up in those adventures. But to tell you the truth I believe it was him. I haven't seen him myself. Maybe I'm too old to believe in ghosts." Richard chuckled a bit, then sobered.

"On your last visit you asked me who will inherit my home. Well, Ms. Walterson, I really don't know. My boys firmly do not want this place, not that they don't want the house. They simply do not want the land with what they call voodoo spirits. And besides, they are all involved in their lives in other parts of the state. They have no use for family history or legacy. That seems to be the way of things. No one cares about carrying on a family name and what that name means. But that's about all we have left. Our name and this scrap of land. And they don't want it."

Richard Barclay bowed his head and over this he wept.

19

WASHINGTON SPRING

"They want scene two cut?" Jimmy was indignant. "Scene two is one of the best parts of the show!"

"I know, but Thomas said it slows down the storyline. We simply need to write a link between scenes one and three," Bryan said.

"If it's so simple, you do it then," Jimmy declared.

"Look, you two. I think we can make this work." Mary Gray was the voice of reason as they sat once more at the table in Bryan and Jimmy's cottage.

"I'm going for a walk," Jimmy declared. He exited with a huff which left the other two to get down to business.

"Welcome to Washington Spring," Bryan shook hands with Thomas Kittering who appeared to be in his late seventies by the severe lines

122

creasing his face. Thomas removed a tweed cap to reveal a totally bald head. He could have been a decade-older version of Bryan who also had a spare look.

"Quite a place here. Allow me to introduce my partner, Joe Taylor." Joe was the smaller of the two men. Both were trim and wore tweed, looking the part of the casual upper class. Thomas carried a leather satchel. Although the two men were quite different in height, the greatest distinction in their appearance was that Thomas was white and Joe was black.

Bryan shook hands with Joe. "Do come in." He stepped back to allow the men into the cottage. "Please make yourselves comfortable."

"I'm embarrassed to ask, but may I use your bathroom? It was a long drive from Baltimore and we didn't see a comfort stop," Thomas said.

"Certainly!" Jimmy suddenly stepped in to play the role of host. "I'm Jimmy, the other half of Bryan. Let me show you to the water closet." Jimmy sauntered off with Thomas following.

"Mr. Taylor?" Bryan said, holding out his hand.

"Call me Joe, please." He grasped Bryan's hand.

"Joe, please meet Mary Gray Walterson. She's our neighbor and one of the writers of *Middle-Aged Madness*."

"Pleased to meet you." Joe extended his hand to her, then turned back to Bryan. "Actually, if you don't mind, I would like to follow Thomas. You should think about adding to the show's line up a redux of Chuck Brown's *Rev it up and Go-Go*. Make it, `When the rest of me can't do much, the bladder is always revved up to go-go.'"

The three laughed.

"We do have a second bathroom," Bryan said.

"I'd be obliged."

Bryan led Joe away.

123

Thomas, white and taller, was the first to return. Bryan was on hand to wave him toward the living room chairs and sofa. "Please, have a seat. May I offer you something to drink?"

Thomas chuckled. "Liquid will just make more trouble, now won't it?"

The four sat.

"The drive was gorgeous. Wish we would've rented a convertible. If I would've known this part of Maryland existed, I might not have been so quick to leave."

"We loved our convertible," Jimmy cooed.

"You were raised here in Maryland?" Mary Gray asked.

"Baltimore City. Tough place. We were there just now to settle my brother's estate. He died last year. Had a storage unit I did not want to open. Painful memories. Didn't help having Joe with me. You have to understand, my brother was a bigot. A racist and a bigot, a troublemaker in and out of jail. I don't know how he lived to eighty. Spite, I guess."

"It's fuel for some folks." Mary Gray remembered her former husband and his vengeful state of mind.

"I never want to do again what I just did. Sort a pile of Southern crap, Dixie banners, Confederate flags, you won't believe it, but white sheets." He hung his head.

"Oh my. That is serious," Mary Gray said.

"Worst part of it is I could never share my life with my family. When I left, I left. Try having a black partner when you're from my family. I changed my last name. Good riddance."

"Ah, Joe," Thomas called as Joe returned to the gathering. "I was just telling these good folks about growing up in Baltimore. And how we couldn't wait to escape."

"You never saw your family again? I mean, once you left?" Mary Gray asked.

"Not mine," Thomas said. "The only reason I had to clean up after my brother was because he saw fit to make a will and leave me everything. If that was a peace offering it came way too late."

"What about you, Mr. Taylor?" Mary Gray asked. She noticed his eyes, deep brown and kind. They crinkled merrily as he talked.

"Call me Joe. I made visits to my father, the man who raised me. But once he died there was no one else."

Joe went on. "Thomas and I met in public school in Baltimore when schools were integrating. It was a terrible time. I was a late-bloomer, raised in Africa, you see. My brother and I came here to live. We were looking for a better life."

"They were stowaways, can you believe it? I tell him he should be the one writing scripts," Thomas added.

"And your brother?" Mary Gray asked.

"He's no longer living," Joe said.

A pall fell over the five.

Thomas filled in the silence. "Why don't we talk about your musical. We really do like the script and the music brings it to life. Let's have a look at your revisions."

"Here you go." Bryan handed the sheath to Thomas.

"Call us old-fashioned, but paper does make for easier reading, at least for these poor old eyes. Thank you for using 14-point type as I asked. Can we move to the table?"

The five shifted to dining chairs so the producers could review the work. Bryan had the keyboard on and ready to play, if needed.

Thomas took off one pair of glasses and put on a different set. As he read he passed pages to Joe who also scanned the manuscript.

"I like what you've done here to connect scenes one and two. And the return to romance in Act Two works better now," said Joe. "It's more authentic after everyone endures the pains of life."

"The closing number will be a show-stopper. Your re-cast of *Stayin'* *Alive* works brilliantly. We love all the songs but that one sealed the deal for us," Thomas said. "I hate to think what the legal eagles will have to do to secure all the music rights for the show, but that's why we pay them the big bucks. Speaking of, I have your contract in my bag." Thomas pulled pages from his leather satchel. "It's pretty much boiler-plate language that we use in all our contracts. You get paid once the show opens and runs."

"I thought we would get paid regardless," Jimmy inserted.

"Sorry. It doesn't work that way. We're all on the hook until the show earns money. But we have you in the contract for $15,000, as we agreed."

"I just thought that you outright bought the script and then we were done," Bryan said.

"This is your first script?" Thomas' tone had a twinge of conde-scension. "Let me explain. You get paid once the show goes on. Which is when we get paid. If we're lucky enough to have a hit on our hands, and I think we will, I've put in a clause to double the $15,000, that is if we reach a certain profit point. It's all in there." Thomas pulled out a pen and placed it in front of Bryan who was now busy reading the contract.

"You can sign it now or later. All three of you."

"I think we'd like to have our resident attorney read through it," Bryan said.

"Fine. As I said, it's boilerplate terms. That's how it's done down on old Broadway."

The next morning Bryan picked up the phone and dialed.

"Ben, would you look over a contract for me?" Bryan asked.

"Sure. What do you have?"

"We've been tight-lipped about this until now. Mary Gray, Jimmy and I wrote a musical."

"You mean like a Broadway show?"

"Yes. And, amazingly, Broadway has come calling. They want to buy it."

"You're kidding."

"I'm serious. Call it connections. Call it luck. We don't have an agent. So, could you look over this contract? The producers were just here and left it."

"They came all the way to Maryland to see you? What kind of musical is this? A new *Phantom of the Opera*?"

"It's a zany tale called *Middle-Aged Madness*. We took familiar songs and re-wrote the lyrics. It's destined to be a hit with our crowd, you know, middle-aged and older? We make aging funny. Or at least relatable."

"Sounds marvelous. Let me see the contract. When do you need it?"

"As soon as you can. We have to get it back to the producers so they can get started."

"Honey, did you see Leena's note? I left it on the coffee table for you to read," Natalie called into Ben's office, their second bedroom.

"No. Does it say anything we don't already know?" Ben shouted over his shoulder into the main living room.

"Here." Suddenly Natalie was behind him.

"Geez. I didn't know you were in here."

"Leena says: `DNA extraction tests proved inconclusive. I sent the remains to the Maryland State Medical Examiner with my report. I doubt we will learn the identity of our man. To the question of burying the bones, they reside with the State. I doubt they will release them to

127

you unless you can claim you are next of kin.' It doesn't look like we will solve our mystery. Ben, are you listening?"

"Yeah. What?" He made a token gesture of turning around.

"Oh, never mind," Natalie said. "Read it when you want."

The doorbell rang. "I'm expecting the luggage back from Tom and Tracie. Can you help me?"

Natalie dropped the page onto Ben's desk as they both moved toward the front door.

20

NEW YORK CITY

"This is just way too exciting for small-town me," Jimmy gushed, flipping one end of his scarf behind himself with a flourish. "I can't believe we're on Broadway," he sang.

"The Lyceum Theatre, no less," Mary Gray chirped. She pulled her coat closer as they strolled from their dinner café to the theatre. It was an early November evening and the weather had turned cold.

"Bright lights. Big city. If only they could see me now!" Jimmy sang.

"Who?" Mary Gray asked.

"Oh, just a dozen brown-noses from Boyden High, my high school in Salisbury, North Carolina. They used to say I was in my element at `Boy's den High.' I thought I kept myself quite disguised. But apparently not," Jimmy clucked. "Mary Gray, who would you most want to see you now?"

"I don't know. My parents, I suppose. My father was like New York, bigger than life, but he was no city slicker. I think he would be proud of me, though. Of us," she added.

"Pete, who would you like to see you now?" Jimmy playfully linked his arm in Bryan's. "Mr. Mod Squad," Jimmy teased.

"I guess my mother. She loved all the musicals. She used to sing to records she'd play on our console stereo. I think she would love this show."

They stopped as one. Before them *Middle-Aged Madness* shone in marque lights. No one spoke.

In awe Mary Gray whispered, "It's real. I mean, it is real." Her voice picked up volume. "We really are here!"

Jimmy linked his other arm in hers and from center position pulled his mates along using dance steps to accentuate his actions. "Let's go!" he sang.

"For God's sake, Joe, why are you so nervous?" Thomas frowned. "You were fine at Dress. It's going to be a hit."

"It's been five years since we put ourselves out there. You know I have trouble at the start of every show. And tonight is Preview night. All those critics."

"Look, the tabs will love it," Thomas reassured him.

"Unless some kid fresh from the latest hip hop does our review."

"We can stand next to hip hop any day. You love this show. I love this show. America is going to love this show."

"At least anyone over fifty." Joe sighed and turned a half-hearted smile up to Thomas. "You always did know how to cheer me."

"And you me. You could have blown me over with a feather when you ran up to me that day in junior high there on the sidewalk. I thought, here is the cutest kid in the whole school coming down the sidewalk to see me."

"You don't know how scared I was."

"You don't know how lucky I felt."

The party backstage began as the thunderous applause ended for the preview performance. Bryan, Jimmy and Mary Gray felt like fish out of water. Crew and cast members all knew one another and laughed at each other's jokes. Bottles were handed from one to another. Bryan made sure to stay out of the way of all alcohol. He wondered if he should have chosen an AA meeting instead of this raucous affair. Surely these professionals had a limit to their consumption since they had to get up and do it all over again.

Bryan was also wary, anticipating more story editing. They had been told that the purpose of Preview night was for the company to perform before a live audience to gauge their response. If no one laughed in the right places it would be up to the writers to fix that.

Joe and Thomas appeared to the three who stood together, apart from the crowd.

"I declare it a smash hit!" Thomas exclaimed, holding out a hand to shake Bryan's. "Not a single re-write needed." Bryan breathed a sigh of relief.

Thomas in turn earnestly shook Jimmy and Mary Gray's hands.

"Now we wait for the reviews," Joe added.

"When will they be out?" Mary Gray asked.

"Tomorrow. Just in time for opening night," Joe answered.

Thomas faced the three writers, "Speaking of tomorrow, come over to our place at one o'clock. I have paperwork we need to go over. Now that we've launched the show I'm sure you'd like to get paid."

At precisely one o'clock Mary Gray, Bryan and Jimmy scrambled out of a cab and mounted the steps of an attractive brownstone.

"You ring," Jimmy said to Bryan. "I'm in awe."

Bryan pressed the buzzer. The three stood shoulder to shoulder.

"Come in, come in," Thomas greeted them and swung open the antique door.

The three entered the brownstone with their mouths agape.

"This is gorgeous," Mary Gray exclaimed.

"We bought when you could still buy in the city without mortgaging your soul. Even then it was plenty. But it's home and we've made it so," Thomas said.

"I'll say," Jimmy added. His eyes fell on a Renoir, wondering if it were an original.

"Come into the study. I believe Joe is in there already."

The three walked through the hallway lined with more French Impressionist paintings.

"They're here," Thomas announced to Joe as they entered a wood paneled room with mahogany furnishings. A large desk faced them with leather chairs fanned out before it.

Joe greeted the trio with warm handshakes beginning with Mary Gray. "Did you get any sleep?" Joe asked with a smile. His dark eyes twinkled.

"Hardly a wink. Too much excitement," Mary Gray answered as their hands clasped.

"Too much champagne," Jimmy added to his handshake. "My head was swimmy all night. The last time I drank champagne was when we decided to write *Middle-Aged Madness*. Last night seemed appropriate to indulge, that is until the bed started spinning."

Bryan took Joe's hand and smiled.

Thomas stood in front of his desk. He opened a folder and indicated a set of papers.

"We agreed you would be paid $15,000 when the show opened. I have a check for you here and a copy of the contract in case you care to review it. Your lawyer friend was smart to negotiate for a future percentage of the house's take seeing that we have a hit on our hands. I trust you read the first reviews?"

The three writers nodded.

"*Here to Stay…Alive!* was the one I liked most," Mary Gray said.

"We liked that, too," Joe said, beaming.

Bryan caught Mary Gray's eye. She shifted her gaze to the contract indicating he should look at the paperwork. Bryan stepped toward the desk.

"Yes, here, have a look." Thomas moved the contract toward Bryan.

Bryan reached into the breast pocket of his new tweed sport coat, pulled out reading glasses and began to review the pages. He came to the back page with their signatures. "What's this?" he scowled.

"What's what?" Thomas asked.

Bryan pulled out an additional page that was stuck to the back of the contract. "This looks to be some kind of report. He read aloud, "'DNA extraction tests proved inconclusive.'" Bryan looked at Thomas who looked bewildered.

"That sounds familiar," Mary Gray said softly. "Bryan, that sounds like the report that Ben and Natalie got on the skeleton they found in the woods."

"Skeleton in the woods?" Thomas asked.

"Yeah. Two of our Washington Spring members were out mushroom hunting and one of them came across some human remains. Bones from a long time ago. They had them sent off for analysis. What does the paper say?"

Thomas took the paper and read the full report aloud. "'DNA extraction tests proved inconclusive. I sent the remains to the Maryland State Medical Examiner with my report. I doubt we will learn the identity of our man. To the question of burying the bones, they reside with the State. I doubt they will release them to you unless you can claim you are next of kin.'"

"That page must belong to Ben. Maybe it got shuffled into our stack when he was reviewing our contract," Mary Gray said.

"Does the rest of the paperwork appear as you remember?" Thomas asked.

Bryan leafed through. "Looks good," he confirmed.

"When will you be going back to Maryland?" Joe asked.

"Saturday," Jimmy sighed. "The life of a church musician. My partner here has to be home to play for church on Sunday."

"It pays the rent," Bryan countered with a small smile.

"But you'll be at tonight's show. Opening night," Thomas declared. "You need to be backstage with us for the Robe Ceremony."

"Broadway tradition," Joe added.

"Everyone involved in the show—and that includes you three— needs to touch the robe for good luck."

"We wouldn't miss it," Jimmy declared.

"We were also hoping you could join us beforehand. We like to have a small plate before the show. Le Marais is near the theatre. Could we meet there at six?"

Mary Gray looked at Bryan who nodded.

"Tell me your intentions, so I'll know what to wear," Jimmy gushed.

Mary Gray rolled her eyes.

"It's casual French. I recommend the beef medallions or duck confit, if you like duck," Joe offered.

"Yummy," Jimmy replied.

134

Thomas handed Bryan the payment. Bryan placed the check and his glasses in his jacket pocket.

"You might take this paper along, too." Thomas indicated the autopsy report.

Bryan nodded and folded it into the other side of his new tweed jacket.

"I'll see you three out," Thomas said, guiding them from his study. "How are you finding our city?" he asked as they returned to the front of the house.

"We love it!" Jimmy announced. "I feel like a bee in honeysuckle. Isn't that one of the expressions your loverboy likes to use, Mary Gray?"

Bryan shot Jimmy a look but with no effect. Jimmy's eyes were on the opulent surroundings.

Mary Gray's stomach lurched. She wondered what Brown was doing while she was two hundred miles away. She wondered if she really cared.

"Have you been to any of the art museums? Or the Museum of Natural History?"

"We've been to St. Patrick's Cathedral and Saint Mary the Virgin...Smoky Mary's?" Jimmy said. "Married to a church musician, you have to realize church is where you spend your time."

"Ah, well, you can give us a complete report at dinner." Thomas opened the door and the three gave their thanks and farewells.

"I see you made it," Thomas said, greeting the three inside Le Marais. The place was filling quickly. "We have a standing reservation here on Thursdays. When you've been in town as long as we have they get to know you."

"Can't eat here Fridays," Joe added.

"Oh?" Mary Gray asked.

"Shabbat," Joe answered. "Start of the Sabbath."

135

"Friday night. Of course," Mary Gray said.

"You are in a town run by the Jewish calendar," Thomas said. "But that need not stop you from enjoying our many churches. You say you visited St. Patrick's and Smoky Mary's?"

"Bryan believes that Smoky Mary's is the highest Anglican church in America," Jimmy said.

"May I take your drink order?" A server came to the table with a pad and pencil in her hand.

"The last good use of paper and pencil," Jimmy said wistfully. "Of course, we did compose *Middle-Aged Madness* mostly using pencil and paper, didn't we, Mary Gray?"

"The usual," Thomas said to the server.

"Same," said Joe.

"Mary Gray?" Bryan asked.

"A glass of your house Chardonnay, please."

"Do you do margaritas?" Jimmy asked. "Just kidding. Do you have any seasonal ciders?"

The server recited the drink list.

"That one with wicked in the name sounds good," Jimmy chortled.

The server nodded. "And you, sir?" She indicated Bryan.

"Coffee, please. Cream and sugar."

The server turned to go.

"So you saw our loveliest churches," Thomas said, picking up the earlier thread of conversation.

"I also want to get to the diamond district. I understand it's not far," Mary Gray added.

"You're a stone's throw away. No pun intended." Thomas chuckled. "Are you planning to make a purchase?"

Mary Gray shook her head. "My father had some blue diamonds. I was hoping to see if any jeweler here carries such things. I'd like to know their worth."

"Blue diamonds?" Joe asked.

"Alluvial blues, I believe they were called."

"Do you know their source?"

"Africa."

"Mary Gray thinks they were smuggled across the ocean," Jimmy added.

Mary Gray shot Bryan a look.

"I only told him after the diamonds went missing," Bryan explained. "He didn't know you had them."

Mary Gray frowned.

"Did you lose them?" Thomas asked.

"I think they were stolen. I only discovered the diamonds recently, hidden in a piece of furniture my father made. There were four. I was going to get an appraisal so I could insure them, but when I went to get them, they were gone."

"What did they look like?" Joe asked.

"They were gorgeous. I don't know how to describe them. The most pure gems you could ever see. My father got them from someone for safekeeping but apparently he never returned them."

"Was your father in London?" Joe asked.

"No. Never. Why?"

"Just wondering. My brother and I—"

The server appeared and set glasses in front of them.

"I'll be back with your coffee," she said to Bryan.

"You three are in for a treat," Thomas began. "Opening night. We decided to include two of your extra songs tonight to see how they work. The orchestra wasn't happy. Extra rehearsal, I suppose. I'm not sure why they're upset since we pay them union wages."

Bryan chafed thinking how easily people assumed that musicians should accommodate changes on the fly.

Reading Bryan's mind Jimmy affected an exaggerated response. "I think they just want to be consulted." Jimmy gestured by throwing his arms outward just as the server came with the coffee.

"Ack!" Mary Gray and Joe shouted as coffee spewed across their necks and backs. The ceramic cup and saucer shattered as it hit the floor.

"I am so sorry," the server said, who instantly knelt to clean it up.

"My fault." Jimmy jumped up and used his napkin to join the task.

Mary Gray and Joe daubed their necks with their own napkins.

"I think I need the restroom," Mary Gray announced.

"Me, too," Joe said.

The two rose from their chairs. Mary Gray followed Joe who knew the way.

In a few minutes they reappeared and looked at each other afresh, having been through the same ordeal.

"That was no fun," she said.

"Did it scald you?" Joe asked.

"I'm not sure."

"Do you want me to see?"

She nodded.

He pivoted her to look more closely at the nape of her neck. His warm hand gently touched her skin.

"Can you feel that?"

"Yes."

"Does it hurt?"

"Mm hum."

"Maybe we should get some ice. Let me see if I can alert the kitchen."

Joe left her standing by the restrooms and returned shortly with a cold towel. He held it on the back of her neck and used his other hand to turn her a little toward him. His hands felt reassuring and his attention comforting, even scintillating.

"What about you? Are you scalded?" she asked.

"I'm okay. I think you bore the brunt of the coffee."

"Jimmy is quite the fellow." Mary Gray smiled at Joe. They were about the same height. His smile was kind and she relaxed into his gaze. The stress of a hundred years seemed to evaporate as she held his eyes. He smiled a funny, almost crooked smile. She opened her mouth to say more, but closed it. She felt a peaceful connection, like they were meant to be here.

"I think I'm okay now," she eventually said.

"Are you sure?"

She nodded, then laughed.

They smiled at each other and held the moment a little longer. Her heart beat faster, a strange sensation racing through her body.

Before the opening night show the three writers along with the directors, producers, cast members, musicians and crew gathered on stage to participate in the Legacy of the Robe ceremony. The garment was covered with insignias of past shows and people's signatures. Following tradition, the robe was presented to a chosen chorus member who, after putting it on, proceeded to walk three counterclockwise loops around the stage while everyone touched it. This ceremony magically ensured the show's good fortune.

"I feel like I'm really part of the inner circle with all these rituals," Mary Gray whispered.

"It's a little like church," Bryan agreed.

After the show Bryan, Jimmy and Mary Gray made their way backstage. The cast was ebullient with a wildly successful opening night. Mary Gray literally bumped into Joe in the midst of the chaos.

"Excuse me," she said as an automatic response. However, she felt an electric sensation as her body touched his. Her mouth opened almost of its own accord.

"Do you have a moment?" she blurted.

"Me?" Joe asked.

She nodded, wondering what in heaven's name she was saying. But she felt a leap of excitement and daring. It was like somebody else had taken control of her body.

Joe looked at her with concern, wondering if something was wrong with the play that she needed to tell him.

"Do you want Jimmy and Bryan here?" he asked.

Mary Gray shook her head. "Can we take a walk? It's too noisy in here."

"Uh. Sure. Let me get my coat," Joe replied.

"I'll tell Jimmy and Bryan I'm stepping out for some air."

When she returned the two pulled on their coats. Joe donned a handsome tweed hat and the two walked toward the theatre's back exit.

"It's cold," Mary Gray declared once they reached outside. She boldly placed her arm through Joe's and pulled him close as if they were two old friends out for an evening stroll. Once more she noticed they were similar in size. She was grateful for his body and its heat.

"November in New York is nothing like what I grew up with in Africa," Joe said after a while to make conversation since Mary Gray was quiet.

"How did you come to be here?" she asked.

"Here in the States or here in New York?"

"Both." Get him talking, she thought to herself. It will buy time to sort out whatever you are trying to do. She wondered if she had lost her mind.

"My brother and I were born in Sierra Leone. When our mother died we decided to leave." Joe was content to let that be that, but Mary Gray indicated for him to go on. At first he didn't say anything, but soon they fell into an easy rhythm of walking, their strides being the same, and he found it possible to say more.

"There was an Englishman who used to come to our place and he told us about England and since we wanted to start new lives we thought maybe we could go there. He took us to Freetown, the port city so we could sail to his country, but, in exchange we had to help him."

Joe paused. He had not told his whole story even to Thomas, only bits and pieces. He was too ashamed to explain the grinding poverty and madness of the place and what he and his brother had to do to escape it. But now the story tumbled out.

"We were actually raised in a mining camp, lots of rowdy men. Our mother didn't let on to my brother and me, but it was clear that what the men said, she had to do. She was beautiful but they couldn't see that. They belittled her, tried to make her weak, but she was strong. She endured their harassment and worse."

Mary Gray blew out her breath.

"We believe she ate some bad meat that made her deathly ill. We were helpless to do anything. After she died, my brother, Nmumba said we had to leave, to get across the ocean, so we agreed to smuggle things."

"Smuggle things?"

"Diamonds, actually, into London. You mentioned your alluvial blues?"

141

"Yes, blue diamonds. They are supposed to be quite rare."

"They are. And four is quite a find. Your father had something very special."

The two were quiet, hearing the sounds of the city.

"How did you get from London to here?" Mary Gray asked. She wanted him to continue talking. She couldn't help herself. She felt like a schoolgirl on a date with her first crush. What was it about this man? He was nothing at all like she imagined herself wanting, as if she even knew what that was. Not to mention he was taken. Clearly taken. And besides that, gay.

"Same way we got from Africa to London, by cargo ship. Sailed into Baltimore. Our very first day a man at the dock asked us to carry car parts to his truck. That man turned out to be the very best man I've ever known. His name was Clarence Taylor. He became my father. He legally adopted me after my brother died."

"You said earlier that your brother died. So young?"

"He was kidnapped by a gang of whites. They were coming for me and they didn't know the difference between us. I hid while they took my brother away. He never came back." Joe pulled away from Mary Gray. She felt suddenly vacant and almost accused.

"The thing is, I know now it was probably Thomas's father."

"What?"

"When Thomas cleaned out his brother's things I saw first-hand evidence of a family's lifelong hatred and insanity. There's no doubt in my mind that Thomas's father was part of the Ku Klux Klan. He passed his hatred on to his oldest son."

Joe paused, remembering.

"In the 1950s with schools integrating, Thomas' father feared that blacks were taking over. So he goaded his oldest son, Roger, to set fire to black people's houses. Thomas overheard his brother's plans and told me. I told my brother Nmumba who then leaked the news to someone who sent thugs to rough up Roger and his gang. Thomas's dad came after me for squealing. And the person they took was Nmumba."

They stopped strolling. Joe stared straight ahead as he spoke.

"It should have been me."

Joe used his sleeve to brush a tear from his eye. Suddenly he could not hold back a tide of emotion and he began to shudder.

Mary Gray led Joe to a bus shelter so they could sit.

"It should have been me," he repeated. He covered his face with his hands.

"I'm sorry," Joe mumbled. "Maybe this is because of opening night. I'm always emotional at the start of a new show. So much at stake. And the older I get, the less I'm able to hide what I feel."

Joe fished a handkerchief from his pocket and blew his nose.

"I wish I knew what to say. You must be so hurt by all of it."

They were quiet.

"What was your brother like? Were you close?"

Joe nodded, absently folding and unfolding his handkerchief.

"Nmumba was my hero. He was tall and strong and he kept us safe. He was my big brother in every way. Since we didn't have family we relied on each other. We sailed the seas together. We stowed away. Never got caught. We fancied ourselves pirates, I think.

Now Joe grew stoic. He stopped fidgeting with his hanky and turned to look at Mary Gray.

"I killed a man over diamonds. Actually, I killed him because I thought he was going to shoot Nmumba."

"Oh Joe," Mary Gray's eyes grew wide.

"We had diamonds with us from Africa—not stolen, mind you—we found them and were trying to sell them. But the jeweler in London got spooked and was going for a gun. Before he could fire, I stabbed him. I became like an animal driven by instinct to protect my brother."

Mary Gray sighed. This was hardly what she expected for her evening out. Whatever was driving her to be with this man, she deeply questioned. Yet, she felt compassion for him. Maybe that was the thing of it—you could care for someone you didn't really know.

Joe looked toward the street and then gazed up toward heaven. What he saw was a streetlight.

"So, you see why the stage became my career. I could create a persona, anything but live the pain of my own life."

Now Joe chuckled.

"Acting coaches are always saying to go deep and imagine yourself in a particular situation. I didn't have to reach very far for anything hurtful. My whole life was fraught with pain. But, it was also filled with joy and love. Clarence loved me like his own son."

Joe wiped his eyes and nose and returned his handkerchief to his pocket. People walked by unaffected by their presence in the bus shelter. Mary Gray was glad no one else had joined them.

"When Nmumba was kidnapped, Clarence didn't know if they were going to come back for me. Clarence took me home. He didn't want me going to school so he had me paint the entire inside of his house. Every room a god-awful shade of blue. It kinda made me blue. But he was right to give me something to do, something to focus on besides the emptiness of my missing brother."

Joe stretched out his legs and crossed his feet. Mary Gray noticed he polished his shoes. In spite of herself she smiled.

"Eventually I returned to school. Thomas and I were in the same grade. He became my lifeline. We had been secretly meeting to read plays. Imagine, a black boy hiding out backstage with a white boy. We fancied ourselves as famous actors doing big productions. After

144

Nmumba's disappearance Thomas and I kept meeting, secretly of course, because we both loved the theatre."

Joe now drew his feet back to himself.

"Thomas got a full scholarship to Juilliard. I was accepted at Howard, both of us in performing arts. After graduating we wound up together. We knew each other secrets, or at least some of them. He had no pedigree and he hated his family. I had no family except for Clarence. I guess I've always thought of Thomas as a replacement for my brother. Don't get me wrong, I love him. I'm not sorry for all the years we've been together. It's been quite a life." Joe looked at Mary Gray and shook his head. "From the stage to producing. We're living the dream. But…"

"But?"

"I could never tell him my whole story. And here I am telling you." He smiled at her.

Mary Gray's heart suddenly sped up. Was he making a pass at her or just being endearing? She mentally scanned his resume: smuggler, stowaway, murderer and married.

"You've had quite a life. I imagine you're going to tell me next that you're a great cook?"

Joe laughed. "Actually, I *can* cook. I'm a very good cook. Ask Thomas."

Mary Gray smirked.

"You think I'm crazy."

"Yes, I do. And I would be too, for all you've been through."

"Tell me about you. Please. I've done all the talking."

"Not much to tell. I worked at the National Archives my whole career. I retired a few years ago and joined Washington Spring. You've been to our Community. You know it's very rural and a bit provincial. The group of us is committed to caring for one another. It's sort of insurance that we will be looked after when we're old and tottering so we won't be turned out onto the street."

"I think it's a great idea. Were you ever married?" He indicated her ringless finger.

"Once, many years ago. My husband drank. He was an angry man. Ours was not a happy home. It was easier not to be married."

"Children?"

"No. I do regret not having children."

"Me, too. But then, so often I would think of my brother and what he sacrificed for me. It just didn't seem right for me to have a full and happy life."

"But you do, don't you?"

"I do, and I don't. Who can say they have everything they want in life? I've received more than I have a right to."

"Would you ever return to Africa?"

He shook his head. "What would make you happy, Mary?"

She pondered his question. "I haven't thought about being happy. I think I am happy right now."

Joe smiled.

When he smiled Mary Gray's insides lit up. She felt tingly. It was as though God had arranged all this so they could meet. Mary Gray suddenly felt what Brown had been saying about her. This all felt so right, so natural, so ordained.

"Do you believe in God?" Mary Gray blurted.

"God?"

Being in the bus shelter here, now with this man felt like the most divinely saturated thing she had ever experienced. She let her silence invite him to answer.

"I do. I guess I haven't expressed that belief very well. Clarence took me to church. I felt love there. Peace. A sense of belonging. I don't go to church any more. Do you think I should?"

Mary Gray chuckled. "I am sure God would be happy to see you. But I'm sure he sees you wherever you are."

"But do you go to church?"

"Every Sunday. Unless there's a snowstorm." She thought about being stuck in Richmond. "I'm on altar guild, I tithe, I do my best to love the Lord. I suppose he does his best to love me." She smiled.

Joe returned her smile. Her insides felt on fire for this man. Was this temptation? Was this love? She could see Flip Wilson with an angel on one shoulder and a devil on the other, wondering if his words "the devil made me do it," were actually true.

"I'll leave the praying to you then," he said, and took her hand.

Mary Gray felt dizzy with emotion as adrenaline pumped through her body. Was she meant to be with this man? Her expression must have revealed her thoughts because she blushed. She sat there looking at Joe like a star-struck lover. The cold of the night no longer registered for all the warmth she felt inside. She was in New York City sitting in a bus shelter falling in love with a man she could never have.

21

WASHINGTON SPRING

"Good night, Mary Gray. Thank you for driving us back from the airport," Bryan said.

Mary Gray parked in her driveway which adjoined Jimmy and Bryan's next door.

"I have trash back here. Do you want me to throw it in the dumpster?" Jimmy asked.

"No, leave it. I'll take it over with mine."

"You're a doll, Mary Gray. Sleep tight!" Jimmy wriggled out from the back of her sedan and pulled a suitcase from the open trunk.

"Bye, Mary Gray," Bryan said. Then turning to face her, "Are you sure you're okay? You seem distant tonight."

"I'm just tired."

"Okay," Bryan said, a questioning look lingering on his face. He removed his luggage and crossed to his and Jimmy's cottage.

Mary Gray gathered the detritus from her car and walked toward the central shed's trash receptacle. As she rounded the building, she heard laughter. The voices sounded like Brown and Angelika. Mary Gray slowed her pace and quietly moved along the shadows in an effort to see what was happening.

"You are a wild man." Angelika was play slapping Brown.

"And you are in need of taming."

"No, YOU are the one who needs taming!" Angelika chortled.

Brown started to tickle her and she playfully screamed.

"Shh—they'll hear you," he sang.

"Stop it. Stop it!" she giggled.

He ceased his torment and the two went inside Angelika's cottage and shut the door.

Mary Gray stood still taking in the scene. So Brown was after Angelika. She probed her heart to ascertain her feelings about this. A twinge of jealousy arose. Brown was obviously on to the next woman. She then wondered if she should warn Angelika he shouldn't be trusted. But how to tell her?

"Brown is going after Angelika." Mary Gray said as she drove to church the next morning.

"What?" Bryan turned to look at Mary Gray from his passenger's seat.

"I heard them giggling last night when I took our trash over to the dumpster.

"Maybe they were just being friendly."

"Not from what I saw. Let's just say they're involved."

"Involved. Okay. How do you feel about that, Mary Gray?"

"I'm worried for her, to tell you the truth. I'm worried that she will fall prey to his sticky fingers."

"Does she have anything he would steal?"

"I don't really know. I should have seen this coming. Apparently he's more like my father than even I realized."

"Why do you say that?"

"Those diamonds I found in my house also included a journal. I discovered that my father had a child by another woman, an out-of-town affair. The child's name is Ursula. Ursula Morton, of *the* Mortons?"

"Ouch. That's a tough one." Bryan let that information hang for a moment. "Do you know anything more about her?"

"No, I don't. Why do you think I threw myself the writing *Middle-Aged Madness*? I needed something to take my mind off that awful revelation." Mary Gray suddenly wondered if her crush on Joe was just a further distraction. Now she worried.

"What just crossed your mind?"

"What do you mean?"

"You look spooked."

"I'm not spooked. I'm just…confused."

"About Brown?"

"No, about Joe."

"Joe?"

"Yes, Joe. He and I took a walk last night."

Bryan was quiet.

"We, I…" Mary Gray lifted her hands from the steering wheel in a gesture of mystification.

"What? You're head over heels in love with Joe?" Bryan asked sarcastically.

Mary Gray said nothing, but smiled.

Bryan looked incredulous. "Mary Gray. He's gay."

"I know he's gay," she snapped.

"And he's married."

She said nothing.

"I see. And you think you're in love with him."

"Bryan, my heart has been such a stranger to me. Do you remember when I first asked you about Brown and how would I know if I loved him? You asked me, Have fireworks started? and I said No. And then you asked if Brown saw fireworks—and I told you Yes? And you said, `He may love you but you don't love him. It's that simple.' I believed you and I should have broken it off with him right then. But my ego so relished that he loved me and I guess I wanted to keep hearing how wonderful I was. But you were right. I didn't love him. Joe? I can't stop thinking about him. The pyrotechnics are in full flame."

"And for him, too?"

"I don't know. I doubt it."

"Joe and Thomas have been together for, what fifty years?"

"Actually sixty."

Bryan's face fell. "And you're going to try to break up that happy marriage?"

Mary Gray was silent.

"I think you're just star struck seeing your name in lights and living the high life that you think you're entitled to pull a man from his house and home." Bryan looked at her intently.

"I hadn't thought of it that way. I was following my heart. Look, I get such precious little information from my heart. Now that my heart's open, yes, I want to follow it. I want to love this man."

"Romantically—"

"Yes. Romantically."

"He's got to be nearly seventy-five."

"He's actually seventy-eight."

"And you think romance is in the air?"

"I don't necessarily mean sex. Okay, maybe sex, cuddling sure. It's about contentment, fit. I have waited my whole life for the right fit. God knows my first husband wasn't it. And during my whole career I never found anyone. I wasn't looking, Bryan. I wasn't. I've been trying to dodge Brown, for heaven's sake."

"When did this happen? I was with you the whole time."

"At Le Marais, when we came out of the bathrooms we just looked at each other and I knew."

"Knew what?"

"That we were meant to be together."

"Great. My spilled coffee brought this out in you. Does he know how you feel?"

"No. And don't worry. I'm not going to tell him. This may just be some astrological alignment that's got me star-crossed. I'm going to resist getting in touch with him, at least until February 14th."

"Well, that's appropriate," Bryan said with a tinge of sarcasm.

Mary Gray smiled. "If it's meant to be, we will both feel it."

152

22

WASHINGTON SPRING

"I've done an analysis of our collective transportation needs." Bryan handed out pages to the gathered group of Washington Spring members at their monthly meeting. "You can see that if we have seven vehicles in the car share program these would cover everyone's needs. There are eighteen of us. We currently have thirteen vehicles. That includes three pickup trucks: Ray, Sandy and Brown."

"Remember, Sandy's is a stick shift," Jimmy added.

Bryan went on. "I'm suggesting that when your vehicles require replacing, that we obtain community cars. We can start a fund that everyone contributes to equally. Then, we begin purchasing one vehicle per year until we have our seven."

"What's the advantage?" Ray asked.

"Fewer vehicles to maintain. Lower car insurance costs."

"How would you insure vehicles so everyone can drive them? Won't that cost more, not less?" Tracie asked.

"I checked into that very question and am waiting for a call back."

"What about maintenance? Who decides when and what needs to be done?" Ray added.

"How about you, Ray?" John B. Martin asked from his place at the head of the table. "Your groundskeeping responsibilities are now being handled by Brown. That leaves you free to take on another form of service to the community. You could keep record of which cars need maintenance and take charge of getting that work done."

"But what about me? I drive a lot more than anyone else. As a nurse, I drive to Baltimore three days a week. I put more miles on a car than all of you combined," Sue Cantelli declared.

"I thought of that, Sue. And you're right. You do drive more than the rest of us," Bryan answered. "Since these cars would belong to the community, they are for the benefit of all, no matter if one drives a little or a lot. Some of you may want to take a vehicle on a trip. I don't think we would restrict usage or track miles and try to allocate costs."

"That doesn't seem fair to me," Tom Allgood chimed in with his mop of red hair. "Tracie and I don't drive all that much, and so we only change our oil once a year. And now we would be paying for vehicles we don't own and to maintain them even though we hardly drive them?"

"What about Christine? She's no longer driving. Do Bill and Christine both have to contribute? It seems like this isn't a very even playing field," Tracie Allgood added.

Bryan deflected their concerns. "Jimmy and I would like to offer to purchase the first shared vehicle as an experiment. Meanwhile, if we can all feed the kitty, we can buy another vehicle next year."

"But if none of us needs to use your—or this—new vehicle, what's the difference?" Tom asked.

"I thought of that. Certain days Jimmy and I would agree not to use the car so others can. That way we can experience the ins and outs of car sharing before taking it on full time."

"I like it," Ray announced. "Give me a fleet of cars. I'll keep 'em humming." He held up his Miller beer can in salute.

"I think it's silly," Sue countered.

John intervened. "Bryan, do you care to make this into a motion?"

"I move that Washington Spring begin a fund where every member contributes one hundred and fifty dollars per month so we can purchase a shared vehicle in one year."

"Is there a second?"

"I'll second it," Mary Gray said.

"Discussion?"

"What about Bill and Christine? Christine's never going to drive again. Why should she contribute?" asked Tom.

"I don't think it's fair," Tracie added.

"Look, when we formed Washington Spring it was to support each other through the aging process. Well, this is one of those sacrifices— we set aside individual gain for the good of the whole," Bryan said.

"That's convenient since it's you two who need a car," rejoined Sue.

"I said, Sue, that Jimmy and I will purchase the first shared car out of our pocket."

Sue sniffed.

Brown watched the proceedings, keeping his thoughts to himself. He was not about to give up or share his truck for anything in the world.

"Come on. Let's get married." Brown pulled Angelika toward him. They were standing in her kitchen, light streaming through the window illuminating her already blonde-white hair.

"Do you mean it?" Angelika asked.

"Sure I mean it. I will carry you over the threshold once you are pronounced my wife."

"Threshold of what?"

"The courthouse, the hotel entrance, this cottage. You tell me!"

"Brown, you really are silly."

"Silly? I'm serious. Look, you're for me and I'm for you. We aren't kids. Why wait?"

"Okay. So what do we do about our cottages?"

"Two can live as cheap as one. I can move in here."

"Here?"

"I spend enough time here so as it is. And you've been to my place. Just a bunch of stuff. Besides, you have better taste than me."

"Do we tell the others?"

"Sure! I want them to know you've made me as giddy as a goat in a boat. After all, if I move in with you don't you think it will be kind of obvious? You're my angel. I just want to be with you. Marry me."

With some effort Brown got down on one knee and took Angelika's hand in his and brought it to his mustached lips. He gazed up at her and waited.

"Why not. I love being with you and life is so much better when you're around," Angelika answered.

"Let's go to the courthouse today."

"Today?"

"To get the license. Once we have the license we can get married in forty-eight hours. We could be married before the weekend."

"Where do we go?"

"Parabar County Clerk's office at the courthouse."

"Okay. I'll get my purse."

"And your ID. I'll get mine and pick you up in my truck in five minutes." Brown stood, kissed Angelika, stroked her white hair and strolled out her front door.

Angelika stared after the closing door, taking in the last moments.

Mary Gray stood just inside the shed getting Christmas decorations when she saw Brown emerge from Angelika's cottage. She surreptitiously watched him trot from Angelika's house to his. Something was up. She could feel it. In two minutes he reappeared in his truck and stopped in front of Angelika's. She came out of her cottage, boarded the truck and in a moment the two were gone.

On impulse, Mary Gray reached into the shed for the universal key. Washington Spring members agreed not to enter each other's cottages unless they had cause for concern. Sue, in setting up the morning monitoring system had only once used the universal key to check on a member who had neglected to place his magnet on his door by ten in the morning. That had been a case of simple forgetfulness and an embarrassed community member faced Sue walking into his house.

Mary Gray took the key from the nail and eyed the Close for any neighbors. Seeing none she hurried over to Brown's cottage. Quickly, she slipped the key in the lock, opened his front door, and shut it swiftly behind her. She felt suddenly awkward looking at the same four walls as her own, but outfitted quite differently. It was a bachelor pad of mismatched furniture, strewn socks, a dirty plate and coffee mugs on a table. Only a potted plant made the place look inviting. She reminded herself why she was here. Diamonds.

Think like Brown, she told herself. Where would he put the diamonds? She entered his bedroom. It contained only an unmade bed and a dresser. She opened the top dresser drawer. Underwear and socks. She felt around for the small diamond wrapper but found nothing. The next

157

drawer was t-shirts. The bottom drawer contained summer shorts. She turned around and looked again at the room. A couple of magazines lay on the floor along with an empty mug. Bed covers were strewn. Her heart hurt to think how differently this man lived compared with Acton who took pride in everything. When he lived here the place was neat as a pin.

She opened the closet door and turned on the light. Jeans and slacks and flannel shirts hung in haphazard array. His hats lay on an upper shelf. Mary Gray felt defeated. Could she be wrong? Or had he simply sold the diamonds and tossed out the *Return to ME* note?

She turned off the closet light, shut the door, then spun around to review the room once more.

Nothing.

Now she went into the second bedroom. Stacks of boxes lined the walls. She lifted a lid. Field and Stream magazines. She went to the next stack and peered into that box. Random souvenirs including a miniature reproduction of the Alamo which she found strange, since its fall represented the loss of Texas' independence. The third set was books, mostly Westerns. She couldn't imagine herself pawing through all these boxes on the chance of finding a tiny slip of paper.

She sighed and decided to check the main bathroom. The medicine cabinet contained nothing out of the ordinary. In the vanity were assorted combs, brushes, clippers, aspirin, and a prescription. She noticed the prescription was for Viagra. Mary Gray rolled her eyes and thought about Jimmy's lyrics for the show, "Now everything's stiff except what should be." She returned the bottle. By the commode she saw another Field and Stream on the floor. A piece of paper stuck out like a bookmark. She stooped over and flipped open the page. It was a letter. Before picking it up, she memorized how it lay inside the magazine.

Unfolding the pages she noticed the legal letterhead, Crumpler, Caton and Williams, Attorneys at Law. She read:

January 23, 2020

Dear Mr. Howard,

I offer sincere condolences on the death of your sister, May Beth Howard. As her executor and attorney, this letter is to inform you that your sister made a provision for you in her will. In preparing her final declarations she was quite sure she wanted her wording to be as follows:

To my brother Wilford G. Howard I leave the entirety of my estate, provided he is married by the time of my death, or by the end of the second year following my death. I make this condition because Wilford will need someone to help him carry the burden of this estate. I do not give it lightly. The ranch will be his, which I know he can run, but the house he cannot keep up without help. I give Wilford my love and thanks for being my big brother. Should he predecease me, or not be married within the allotted time, I request that the ranch and my estate's holdings be sold and the proceeds given to St. Jude's Hospital for Children.

To claim your sister's estate, I will need to see proof of your marriage by the end of the next calendar year. I am prepared to discuss the details of your sister's wishes and answer any questions.

I am sincerely yours,

H.R. Williams, esq.

Mary Gray gaped. It all became clear, crystal clear. The man was on the hunt for a wife. She felt sick. All his platitudes, his compliments, his playful affection, all lies. Deceit and lies. She read the letter again and noted the date. It was almost the end of the second year and Brown had one month left to marry. He was doing a good number on Angelika. Mary Gray needed to warn her. But how? She would have to expose that she had read the letter. She was caught in a trap of her own making. She folded the letter and returned it exactly as it had been in the magazine. Her missing diamonds now seemed secondary. With a heavy heart she went through the motions of peering into additional drawers. She made a cursory pass through his kitchen and once more glanced around the living room. No sign of her jewels but she had certainly found something of great value.

"He never loved me," Mary Gray declared to Bryan. The two were splitting the overnight watch at Bill and Christine's cottage. Bryan had arrived only to slump onto the couch looking too tired for his upcoming shift. Mary Gray was in an upholstered chair with her feet on an ottoman, a book resting in her lap.

"What do you mean?" Bryan asked wearily.

"Brown. He never loved me. He was posing. He needs to marry before the year is over to claim his deceased sister's estate."

"You're kidding. How do you know this?" Bryan was now alert and interested.

"Let's just say I did a little snooping."

"Mary Gray?"

"I took the shed key and went in his house while he was out with Angelika. Now I know why he's all over her. He has a letter from his sister's attorney. She left him her ranch and who knows what else. But she made it conditional on him being married, that he will need a wife to

160

help him run the whole shebang. I know that's true. He's certainly a capable outdoorsman, but his sister is right. One look at his place confirms it. He has no housekeeping sensibilities."

"I wouldn't dismiss his feelings for you as totally bogus. He seemed genuine to me."

"He probably took acting classes before cowboying on the open range."

"Hold on. Let's just think about this. The man who has probably never had a single acting class in his entire life, you want to dismiss as being a total fake, while you swoon over a man who is not only a seasoned actor, but makes his entire living painting fantasy scenes for others."

"Come on, Bryan. That's not fair."

"It *is* fair. You think Brown's a liar and a cheat."

"He IS."

"You have no hard evidence he stole your diamonds. You go snooping and you find a letter. You put two and two together and believe he never loved you and that he's now interested in Angelika only because she is his ticket to acquiring his sister's estate. You didn't love him, Mary Gray. I don't know that I wouldn't have moved on to greener pastures."

"But what about the diamonds? How did he afford to move here?"

"He told you he had resources you didn't know about. Maybe he owns oil wells. He's from Texas, you know."

"You're impossible, Bryan. I'm not sure you're even my friend."

Mary Gray gathered her belongings and left.

Late in the morning Mary Gray awoke and immediately went to her front door to put out her bird magnet. She shivered as cold air flowed through the open door. In spite of the temperature, she couldn't help but step outside far enough to survey the Close for Brown's truck. It was gone. Two days earlier Mary Gray saw Brown and Angelika leave. They had returned, but now seemed to be away. If they were gone for any length of time they would have had to let Sue know since she was the magnet maven. Mary Gray retreated inside, washed up quickly and went across the Close to see Sue.

She knocked.

"Hi Mary Gray," Sue's husband Sandy answered the door. "To what do we owe the pleasure?"

Mary Gray suddenly realized she needed to invent a reason. She stalled.

"Is Sue around?"

"She's in the shower getting ready for work. Can I help?"

"Actually, maybe you can. We have some items at church that may need to be moved and Brown's truck is large enough to do the job. Do you happen to know where he is?"

"Sue said he phoned and told her that he and Angelika would be traveling together and wouldn't be back until next week."

"Next week?"

"I'm sure I'm not supposed to tell, but I think it's a honeymoon."

"A honeymoon?"

"I gather you two were just friends, you and Brown, but he's grown quite fond of Angelika. He said they were going to be married at the Parabar Courthouse and take a little trip, so not to expect them to be around."

"Which day are they getting married?"

"I believe today. At noon today. I don't know if I'm talking out of turn here. Sue said he sounded happier than, how did he put it, than a Junebug on a tomato? Something like that."

"Sandy, I'm going to need to dash. I appreciate you letting me know." She turned to make a hasty exit.

"Hey, if you need my truck, just let me know. I'm happy to—" Sandy started to say, but Mary Gray was gone.

"Damn. Damn. Damn!" She looked at her watch. 10:40. Mary Gray scrambled to get her keys and purse. Inside her car she backed out haphazardly, nearly running into Tom and Tracie walking their dog. She even burned a little rubber pulling onto the road.

She thought out loud while she drove. "What will I use as an excuse? I'm at the Courthouse doing some archival work? How interesting to bump into you?" She chided herself. Even if she could come up with a plausible reason for being there, how could she stop them from getting married? Or more like, how could she explain to Angelika the motive behind Brown's proposal? She would tell Angelika that her dress was torn, that she must come to the Ladies Room right away. There she would tell Angelika the truth, that she suspected Brown of stealing her diamonds, that in trying to find her jewels she happened to run across a letter in Brown's place that his sister left him her estate, but only if he married by the end of this year. She would reveal herself because her transgression was far smaller than his. Surely Angelika would see it that way, after all she was rescuing Angelika from a disastrous decision.

Resolved, Mary Gray pressed the accelerator and flew across the country road. She prayed she would arrive in time.

Pulling into the lot Mary Gray saw Brown's truck. Her heart sped even faster. They really were here! She climbed from her car and hurried across the sidewalk. The clock in the courthouse tower showed 11:25.

Inside the Courthouse a guard stopped her to be screened. As she emptied her overcoat pockets and dropped her purse in a plastic bin she quizzed the man in uniform.

163

"Where would someone get married in the Courthouse? I'm here to—help." Mary Gray stumbled over her words.

"Beats me. I'm not a county employee. I'm just Security. Check the directory." The guard pointed to the wall.

Mary Gray hastened to it. Courtrooms, meeting rooms, offices, nothing about wedding chambers. She whirled around trying to find someone helpful. Just then she heard Brown's booming voice. She looked up the stairs. Brown and Angelika were coming down arm in arm, smiles on their faces.

"This calls for the best lunch in town," he exclaimed. "Guard," Brown called across the open room, "where is the best place to eat in town?"

"Beats me," the guard replied. "I'm just Security. I bring my own."

Mary Gray gaped as they walked out the door, never seeing her as they went.

23

WASHINGTON SPRING

Throughout Christmas Mary Gray tried to focus on her own life. Six weeks remained until she planned to call Joe. She told herself she would use this time to sort out her feelings for him so she could explain herself, if it still seemed appropriate. Since they had no communication, she had no way of knowing if he had been thinking of her as she was of him. Her heart always came back to sadness. How could she dare to hope that Joe might love her? His leaving a relationship of sixty years was preposterous. Besides, what kind of person would he be if he did? And what could she offer him, anyway? On New Year's Eve she decided it wasn't worth the effort to sort her confused feelings because knowing how deeply she felt wouldn't matter. Any hope for a life with Joe was doomed. Mary Gray felt utterly alone.

~~~

"It's New Year's Day, Mary Gray. Come on over!" Jimmy sang into the telephone.

"I don't feel much like celebrating."

"Come on, now. It's a brand new year. We have the whole 365 days ahead to make of them what we will."

"You two go on."

"Bryan's been missing you."

"Yeah?"

"Yeaah," he exaggerated his answer. "Come on. Let's mend these fences. It was bad enough that you two spent Christmas avoiding each other, and you two call yourselves Christians," Jimmy huffed.

Mary Gray bristled. "Has he said anything?"

"Just that he hasn't a single friend in the world anymore, and don't think I'm not offended by that!"

Mary Gray laughed. "I see."

"I mean, what good are Linc and Pete if there's no Julie?"

"Okay. I'll come over. What time?"

"That's the spirit. Come by at four. We'll have dinner ready and show tunes on."

Jimmy made it easy for Bryan and Mary Gray to reconcile—he put on their favorite musical, *The Sound of Music*. Afterward, Bryan walked Mary Gray home which was ten steps from his own.

"Thanks for coming over. I know it was hard to break the ice. I'm glad you did."

"Me, too. It sure is dark. I'll be glad when the days look like they're getting longer. Sweet spot," Mary Gray mumbled.

"Sweet spot?"

"Something Brown said about the open range, when the days are longer but not too long. He called it the sweet spot."

"Mary Gray, I think you miss him."

"Maybe I do. Maybe what I really miss is his doting on me. Who wouldn't miss that?"

"I'm sure it doesn't help with Angelika and Brown being happy as clams."

Mary Gray nodded.

"What are you going to tell Joe?"

"I don't know, Bryan. This cooling off time is necessary. I'm sure for me this was just a momentary heartthrob, even if it did feel real. I mean, who would give up sixty years with someone at this stage of life? And what would that say about them, anyway?"

Now Bryan nodded.

"I love the idea of being with him. But I can't set myself up for yet another heartbreak. I've had three already, my father, my ex-husband, and Brown. Aren't most people out of the game after three strikes?"

"Just for the inning. The game isn't over, Mary Gray. Trust me."

"It is for me."

Mary Gray's phone rang at one in the morning. Her first thought was to wonder if she was due at Bill and Christine's and had overslept, but then she remembered that her shift wasn't until next week. She looked at her phone. Joe. She snapped it up and answered.

"Joe?"

"Mary. Forgive me. I—I didn't know who to call. You're a praying a person. I thought maybe you could help."

"How? What can I do?"

"I'm at St. Luke's-Roosevelt and they want me to decide whether to extend Thomas's life.

"Oh Joe. What happened?"

"We were coming out of the theatre and he fell ill, stricken, really. It was quite a scene. Medics came and brought him here. If I tell them not to give him life support, he's probably going to die. If I tell them to hook him up, he may survive."

"What do you think you will do?"

"He and I have been partners our whole lives. Our whole lives, Mary. Except for a few young years, we were always together." Joe began to sob.

"Oh Joe," Mary Gray sighed.

"I can't be alone with this decision."

Mary Gray looked at the clock. There was no time to drive there. No time to fly.

"Then let's pray," she suddenly said.

"Yes, you pray."

She collected herself and breathed deeply. "Lord, you are always ready to give and your servants Thomas and Joe need you and your direction. You know their situation. God, grant Joe the gift of insight to discern your will."

Mary Gray paused hoping God was hearing their prayer and would answer her petition.

She went on. "If you are calling Thomas home, please take him sweetly and hold him as your own child. Fold him in your arms. Let him know that he is home in you. If it is not yet time for him, grant Joe and the doctors everything they need to revive Thomas that he may continue on this earth to do what you have for him to do."

She could hear Joe whispering, "Please, God, please."

"Lord, hear us as we pray, for we know that in life and in death you are with us. In Christ Jesus we pray. Amen."

Mary Gray heard voices through Joe's phone.

"Mr. Taylor? We need to know what to do."

"Leave it to the Lord. God will either call him home or bring him back to life. Do not put him on machines. It's not his will."

Mary Gray wondered whether Joe meant God's will or Thomas'. In the end, it didn't matter. Thomas died within the hour.

Joe texted her early the next morning. "Thank you for last night. He's gone."

24

WASHINGTON SPRING

"Broadway honored Thomas Kittering in grand style. The Actors' Equity Association held a memorial gathering where actors and stage managers recalled Thomas' long reach into their lives. The New York Times did a full spread tribute to Kitterings' influence on 19th and 20th century stage productions. The Times highlighted *Middle-Aged Madness* as evidence that Thomas Kittering had remained vitally involved with the theatre and was hardly done with his life's work. Television shows, magazines, radio hosts and reporters all offered to interview Joe, but Joe only did the minimum. He knew Thomas loved the spotlight, so let him be the one to shine, is how Joe thought about it. Besides, he was busy keeping the show running, for as the old saying went, *The show must go on!*

~~~

Unable to keep her fingers from dialing, Mary Gray called Joe. The moment he answered she realized she hadn't prepared what to say.

"Mary?"

"Hi Joe. I wanted to check on you." Did that sound plausible?

"I'm okay. Thanks for asking."

"Are you keeping busy?" Why was she asking him that?

"I'm at the theatre most nights. Tickets are sold out for six months, can you believe it?"

"Will you be having a service for Thomas?" She was fishing for a reason to come to New York.

"Not a traditional service. He wasn't religious. He let the theologians debate and speculate. He was agnostic, actually."

"Will he be buried?" If not a service, maybe Joe would want others to be with him for some kind of internment.

"He's been cremated. I asked for permission to place his ashes in a shoe worn by Elaine Stritch from our first production. Thomas adored her. I'm having the ashes and shoe bronzed and placed in The City Museum. The curator there is helping me."

"I wish I could help," she said, truly wanting some reason to be with this man.

"You are dear, Mary. Thank you for thinking of me. I'm sorry but I do have to dash. Let's talk another time."

They said goodbye.

Mary Gray replayed their exchange and wished she could have re-written it a hundred ways. Her questions must have sounded like an interrogation. She hung her head, wishing she hadn't called at all.

~~~

"We need a hand count for this vote," John announced. The next Community meeting was underway with all members squeezed into John's cottage.

"Christine shouldn't vote," Tracie said.

"Sure she can. She's not been declared incompetent," Bill retorted.

"Then why are we splitting shifts at your house?"

Bill looked John's way.

Sue spoke up. "Dementia takes many forms. In some patients—"

"Put a sock in it, Sue," Ray mumbled.

"I'm just trying to explain."

John cut in. "May I remind you that we are here to support each other. That is the basis for our charter. Christine is still a voting member until a doctor says otherwise." John was aware that Christine was present and listening.

"I'm not marbleless," Christine called out.

John resumed. "We have a motion on the floor to begin a pilot program for car-sharing that includes purchasing one vehicle from combined funds. To create that fund, every Washington Spring member will deposit one hundred and fifty dollars a month into a common purse starting the fifth of next month. All members in favor please raise your hand."

Eight hands went up including Christine's.

"Those opposed?"

Nine hands went up.

"As the chair, I do not vote unless there is a tie. All votes are now accounted for. Mary Gray, do you have what you need for your records?"

"Yes."

172

"The motion fails."

Bryan sat back and exhaled. Why did he think living in a community was going to be fun?

That night Angelika was on first shift at Bill and Christine's cottage. She glanced at her watch. Midnight. She looked around their home with expensive furnishings and a pretty pot of flowers.

She thought back to her massive gardening week. Even after filling her house and yard with plants and flowers she still had more flowers and pots than she had rooms.

"I think I will take one of you to Bill and Christine's and the other of you over to Brown's," she had said to a pair of violets. She smiled wondering if Brown would take offense at violets, although she knew that violets were anything but weak and limpid.

She had walked across the Close with the two flower pots in hand, dropping off the first one at Bill and Christine's. Chris answered the door and brightly smiled to see Angelika. The two women didn't often have a chance to chat anymore and Angelika promised she would try to return later.

When Angelika reached Brown's house she realized his truck was gone. In spite of the obvious, she knocked. Hearing no response, she tried the door. It was unlocked so she let herself in. This was not her first time seeing his house. However, it was the first time she was there without him. It looked shabbier than she remembered, perhaps because he was so large and commanding that everything else retreated to the background.

"Here, let's find you a nice sunny spot," she had said and started looking through his rooms. Pausing at his bathroom she set down the flowers to make her walk-around easier. When she returned to pick them up she saw the pot had dripped dirty water onto his countertop.

Searching for a sponge but finding none, she tore off an ample supply of toilet paper. That's when she saw an envelope by the commode. It looked to be from a law office. She wondered who would be writing to him from a legal outfit. Not my business, she had thought, and cleaned up the mess. As she flushed the paper down the toilet her eyes fell once more on the return address: Crumpler, Caton and Williams, Attorneys at Law.

Bringing her attention back to her surroundings, Angelika focused on the pot of violets at Bill and Christine's. Marrying Brown had not been so hard. It made sense, even if it were dollars and cents, considering she had likely averted a total financial meltdown.

25

WASHINGTON SPRING

"*Middle-Aged Madness* continues to thrill audiences," Joe texted to Mary Gray. "The tabs keep rolling in with positive reviews."

Mary Gray's heart thumped as she read his text. Her fingers shook as she typed her response.

"Thank you for telling me. Would you come to Washington Spring? We are having a party. It's for my birthday."

"When?" he typed.

She let out a little yip.

"Next Saturday."

"What time?"

"4:00"

Silence followed. Her elation began to sag. Find something to do she told herself, but nothing was large enough to eclipse her awareness that their communication had ended. Had she been too obvious? Too pushy? Wouldn't a friend ask another friend to a party?

Her phone suddenly blinked to life. "Sure."

"Wonderful! It's my 70th birthday," she replied.

"I remember 70. LOL"

"We will be at St. James Episcopal Church, Parabar Shore."

"I will put it on my calendar."

Mary Gray let the conversation rest. She felt like a school girl with a crush on someone who hardly knew she existed. Why was she so head over heels for this man? He held nothing for her. We'll be friends, she consoled herself, but she knew in her heart that would be settling for small rations at a feast she yearned to enjoy.

"Let me get your buttons. Stand still, please. You are like a wiggle worm." Jimmy held hair pins in his teeth and used his fingers to fasten the back button loops of Mary Gray's dress. It was coral colored in a style that flattered her medium-size frame.

"Those flowers should hold in your hair if you keep still."

"I'm nervous," Mary Gray said. Weeks earlier she confessed to Jimmy about her feelings for Joe, though she suspected Bryan had already clued him in. She loved that Jimmy also knew Joe and could on some level relate to her swooning.

"Mary Gray, we are due at the church in twenty minutes. You really are making this impossible," Jimmy chided. "There. I have you button-ed. I hope you don't need to take this off quickly," he smirked.

Mary Gray rolled her eyes.

"I'm using the bathroom and then we *must* go," Jimmy chirped.

Mary Gray looked in her bedroom mirror once more. In her hair were delicate flowers. At last she had something to smile about. She felt as though her whole life was about to change. And she wanted it to.

That was the miracle. She had not even realized how stagnant she had become. How clearly she could see her old life, ready to be shed like a snake skin. She reached into her jewelry box for the last item to put on, earrings once belonging to her mother in the same coral color as her dress. At the side seam of her jewelry box she saw a small piece of paper. Pulling it out she read the familiar words *Return to ME*. Pressing deeper into the seam she felt hard stones. Working these into her fingers she pulled out the four alluvial blue diamonds.

They were here. The whole time, they were right here. How had she missed them? She sank to her knees in prayer.

Mary Gray's birthday party was held in the church hall. Jimmy had wound silk flowers around the heavy draperies pulling them back to let natural light stream into the large room. Bryan piped in music from their show to elevate the mood. A colorful banner read *Mary Gray is Splendidly Seventy!* Round tables dotted the room with food and flowers. The guests included all the Washington Spring residents, church members and even Richard Barclay who had dressed up and come out. She half expected him to bring his hunting dogs. Mary Gray made her debut quietly and began circulating among the various groups.

Before moving to a new group, Mary Gray stood alone scanning the room. Bryan approached her with a glass in his hand.

"For you, Queen of Sheba." He handed her a champagne flute.

"I thought I was Julie, Mr. Mod Squad."

"Today, my dear, you are royalty." Bryan bowed, took her hand and whispered, "You look marvelous."

She blushed as Bryan released her hand and retreated.

One face was missing.

Brown and Angelika approached Mary Gray.

"You look prettier than sunshine on a chilly morning," Brown exclaimed. He bent down and kissed Mary Gray on her cheek. His mustache tickled.

"Thank you, Brown," she said. For the first time Mary Gray felt nothing for Brown, good or bad, nothing conflicted at all. In fact, she felt released of the relentless tug of war between her head and her heart where he was concerned. She was certainly glad she hadn't accused him of being a thief.

"You look lovely," Angelika added.

"I hope you two are enjoying married life," Mary Gray said.

"Happy as oysters on the whole shell," Brown declared.

Since no one could come up with any further small talk the pair simply smiled and moved on to one of the food tables.

"Sunshine," someone said. Mary Gray whirled around to see Joe behind her removing his sunglasses. "Maybe I should leave these on," he mused, indicating either her or the bright room. She hoped he meant her.

Reflexively, Mary Gray embraced him. They fit perfectly, neither too big nor too small. Made for each other. Her heart leapt to her throat.

She forced herself to release him.

"I'm delighted you're here," she managed. "How was the drive? Would you like something to eat or drink?"

"I'm fine for the moment, thank you. Glad to find you, actually."

Just then Ben and Natalie appeared. Mary Gray wasn't sure whether to be relieved from her babbling or annoyed to share this precious moment. Remembering her manners she offered introductions.

"Ben, Natalie, please meet Joe Taylor. Joe produced *Middle-Aged Madness*. He's just driven down from New York City."

"I'm Ben Lebowitz. Good to meet you." The men shook hands.

178

"I'm Natalie, Ben's better half," Natalie mused, also taking Joe's hand.

"We are so sorry to hear about your partner. What a tour de force you two have been for the theatre."

"Thank you," Joe demurred.

"I hear the show continues to be a raging success, taking Broadway by storm. Natalie and I mean to see it," Ben continued. "We just need to make time to do it. We keep wanting to get back to the city."

"You can't imagine how busy we are." Natalie turned to Mary Gray. "I told Ben I hope that you can develop some new passions for yourself, like we have."

"What, like mushroom hunting?" Ben mused as he looked at his wife.

"For one, yes. Just be prepared that anything might turn up. Even bones," Natalie added for dramatic effect.

Ben eyed his wife.

"I meant to ask. Did your friend ever identify those bones?" Mary Gray inquired.

"No, she said they were probably someone who had met an unfortunate end." Natalie leaned in and whispered. "Might have been a lynching."

Joe turned to Natalie. "A lynching?"

"Such unpleasant talk at a party. Geez, Natalie," Ben scolded.

"She asked," Natalie retorted.

"You said a lynching. You found bones of someone who was lynched here in this area?" Joe asked.

"Well, not here, here. In a field not far from Washington Spring. Actually, not far from *the* Washington Spring, the brook named for George Washington. Anyway, we were mushroom hunting and—"

Joe looked at Ben. "Are you the attorney whose paper got shuffled into the show's contract? Please, tell me what you know," Joe said.

Ben picked up the story. "The forensics were inconclusive. An anthropologist friend of ours ran tests on the bone shards and skull pieces we found. She said it was a teenaged African American male, and that because the jaw had been fractured and there was no grave marker, that this *could* have been a lynching. The bones weren't old enough to have been an enslaved person. She said if the bones had been that old, nothing would have been left by this point. But these were probably at least fifty years old."

Joe's face froze.

"My brother, Nmumba went missing sixty years ago. Men came and took him away. We never saw him after that."

"Could the bones be your brother?" Natalie's eyes widened.

"Where are these bones now?" Joe asked.

"Leena had to turn them over to the State of Maryland," Ben answered.

"We asked her if we could give them a proper burial, but she said the State had a right to them, unless next of kin could claim them," Natalie added.

"If this was Nmumba, it would mean everything to me to collect his bones and have him with me once more."

The four stood staring at one another.

"Let me know what you find out," Joe said as he and Mary Gray reached his black BMW. An air of awkwardness descended. How would they say goodbye? Mary Gray stood still willing herself not to reach for him.

Joe turned to open his car door but it had locked in the time they were talking. He fumbled his keys and they dropped to the ground. He and Mary Gray simultaneously reached down. Their hands touched. Mary Gray allowed her fingers to linger on his an extra second. As they stood she looked into his merry, brown eyes. He looked into her grey-green eyes. Heaven. This felt to her like heaven.

Joe broke their gaze. He moved to kiss her on the cheek. Mary Gray tilted her face to catch his lips but it was a most awkward miscon-nection, their lips not quite touching. She felt horribly embarrassed. He withdrew, reached for his door and slid into his car.

Mary Gray watched him go, and as she did she wished that some-thing, even hell would open and swallow her.

"Joe, I need to apologize." Mary Gray said. She suddenly wished she were talking on her old princess phone so she could twist and twirl its long cord. Instead, she reached for a notepad and started to doodle to relieve her nerves.

"If I lose you it's because I'm about to enter the tunnel," Joe said.

"Look, I didn't mean to…" to what? she thought. "to make you feel awkward. I just…"

"It's okay, Mary. I should have said something to you."

"Like what?"

"Like I'm not the on the market."

Mary Gray was speechless. Was she so obvious?

"I should have been a bit more bold, but I wasn't sure what to say. I'm glad you had me come down, but I don't want to impose on you."

"Impose on me?"

"I mean, I don't want to give you the wrong impression."

"I can't expect you to fall in love with me. I mean, look at me. I'm over the hill, dreadfully droll, and, well, you're gay."

"Mary, I've been thinking that my—"

"Joe? Joe?"

The tunnel.

181

She had a chance to collect herself. Was she actually admitting openly that she had feelings for him? She had schooled herself on playing it cool. No one liked a come-on.

"Mary, can you hear me?" He was out of the tunnel.

"I can hear you."

"I shouldn't lead you on."

"I was that obvious?" She couldn't get her mouth to follow the script.

Joe chuckled. "I love you, Mary. I will be in your debt forever. You were there for me when Thomas died."

"But I wasn't. All I did was pray."

"Your prayer helped clarify my decision. I'm a lonely old man, that's true. We should be good friends. We already are."

"I know. I'm sorry."

"No, I'm the one who's sorry. Let's be close friends." He emphasized the word friends.

"Almost nothing better in the world," Mary Gray replied.

26

WASHINGTON SPRING

Brown stood looking toward the field behind Angelika's cottage, a coffee mug in hand. "So this is where the pony appeared?"

"It liked our field. Every day I led her out from the shed and she contented herself just to graze on the grass. Amazingly, she didn't run away."

"That's some kind of miracle she made it back to Alice's." Brown sighed. He set down his mug and turned to his wife. "I think it's time you know."

"Know what?"

"I am the beneficiary of my sister's estate. It's quite large."

Angelika appeared surprised.

"Now that we're married, what's mine is yours."

Angelika smiled.

"However, it's in Texas. It includes ranchlands, herds, and a house. And not too shabby of a house. We have to decide if we want to keep it."

"It sounds like your dream come true!"

"In many ways it is. My sister's husband was a ranch man and he kept good men on it. The men are still there looking out for the place. I can sell it, rent it or we can move into it."

"Perhaps I should see it?"

"I was hoping you'd say that. Once you get some Texas air back in your lungs, I think you will agree it's better to be in Texas."

"I told you you'd love it here!" Brown exclaimed. He had Angelika tour the ranch on horseback. The pair now trotted toward one of the barns. Dismounting, they led their horses to water.

"I do love it," Angelika said, happy to be in the sunshine.

Brown began some barn chores. Angelika leaned at the doorway, half inside, half out. "Brown?" she began.

"Hmm?" He had a brush in his hand.

"Brown, would you come here?"

He put down the tool and walked over. He was so much taller than she was that she almost lost her nerve.

"I need you to know something that may make a difference in the decision about moving here or staying in Washington Spring."

"What's that?" She had his attention.

"I don't think I have the financial footing to keep on at Washington Spring. I thought I did when I applied. I should have had enough money to see me to the end of my days, but the lawyer didn't explain that I would have to pay a large state inheritance tax. That bill put a huge dent in my account. I'm actually just about broke." She held her breath and waited for his reaction.

184

His gaze upon her grew stern. Her heart began to pound.

"Well, then welcome to your new home," he announced, his face breaking into a grin. Brown picked her up and whirled her around. Lowering her to the ground he embraced and kissed her.

27

WASHINGTON SPRING

Mary Gray put down the letter and telephoned Joe. It was an entire year since the show had opened and she had fallen for this lovely and unavailable man. She was glad they were friends and prayed daily to be released of her obsession. After all, Joe had made his position clear. It had helped to focus on projects which included confirming the identity of the bones. Mary Gray had sent a copy of Joe's one photo of Nmumba to Leena who used the picture and her professional position to petition the State of Maryland. Leena made the case that the bones were in fact Nmumba.

Over the phone Mary Gray told Joe the wonderful news.

"They agree to release the bones to you on the grounds that the probability is high that you are next of kin." Mary Gray ached to see Joe's face.

He was quiet.

Finally he said, "I want my brother with me."

"Would you return him to Africa?"

"No. He wanted only to be away from Africa. Our mother's bones may be there but her spirit lives with the heavenly spirits."

"Richard Barclay believes your brother's spirit still dwells in the woods on his land. He told me his sons twice encountered a black boy asking for directions to Baltimore, like a spirit trying to find his way home."

"Then we must ask Richard Barclay if we may walk his land and catch my brother's spirit so he can be brought to peace. If anyone can bring him home it would be me."

The next week on a Thursday, corresponding to the day of the week that Nmumba was kidnapped, Mary Gray and Joe carried Nmumba's bones in the small African sweet grass basket she received from Acton. With Richard Barclay's permission, they strolled his field and woods. As they went, Joe became his native Yusuf and sang a low, mournful chant calling in Krio to Nmumba's spirit.

> *Come home, come home to where our people rest.*
> *Leave earth, leave earth, give no resistance,*
> *for with the heavenly beings belongs your existence.*

A chilly breeze swept through the field and drops of rain began to fall. Yusuf sang louder as the breeze blew into a wind. In spite of the cold, Yusuf lifted his head toward the sky, tears mixing with the scattered raindrops. His body shook with grief as he remembered his sturdy and faithful brother holding his hand, sharing his bread, guiding them to the place he thought would be better for them. As Yusuf wept he held

187

the sweet grass basket above his head, still chanting, still singing. Gradually the wind slowed and a weak sun began to appear.

"You heard me, my brother. You heard me. You are now at peace. You are now at peace."

Yusuf lowered the basket. His arms felt heavy with age yet light with exultation and conviction.

He turned to Mary Gray. "My brother is finally home. He now rests with our ancestors. He has confirmed this for me, that all is well."

Mary Gray opened her eyes from praying. She, too, felt a stirring in her heart she hoped was Nmumba's release.

"He is gone. He is gone. He is gone." Joe wiped his eyes. "We may bury these bones, Mary. They no longer contain my brother's spirit."

Two days later they stood in the small yard behind Joe's New York home. Joe raised a shovel and plunged it into the dirt. He grunted, realizing it took more strength than he expected. Mary Gray's first thought was to help, to take her own turn rending the soil. But she caught herself. This was Joe's work. He tried again, this time using a different angle. The land resisted, not wanting to yield. Mary Gray wondered if this had some deeper meaning. Maybe Nmumba didn't want to be buried. But, as Joe said, the bones no longer held Nmumba's spirit. She stood back and watched as Joe tried again.

"It is as though he is saying to me, `Little Brother, life is not easy. It was never easy for us. Why should it be easy now?'"

The dirt began to give as Joe continued to stab at the earth.

"Probably frozen," he said.

When Joe finally made an opening about the size of a large shoe box he stopped and stepped back.

"I think it is ready."

Mary Gray picked up the sweet grass basket they had brought with a small pouch she had laid in the basket beside the bones.

"Are you certain you want to do this?" Joe asked.

She nodded.

Joe carefully knelt by the hole, feeling the ache of age in his body.

Mary Gray removed the pouch and handed him the basket. She put her hand on his shoulder, then crouched down until she was on her knees beside him.

Joe solemnly picked up the bones of his brother, every last shard, every little piece and held them in his hands.

Without a word, simply knowing they would do this together, they simultaneously lowered their precious possessions into the hole, the bones of a brother and four blue diamonds with a slip of paper that said *Return to ME*.

Made in the USA
Columbia, SC
09 April 2022

58520993R00111